Kate Petty is the author of many books for
children – pop-up books and non-fiction as
well as stories. She lives in London with
her husband. They have a son and a
daughter.

The Girls Like You Series

Sophie
Hannah
Maddy
Charlotte
Holly
Alex
Josie
Zoe

Josie

KATE PETTY

Dolphin Paperbacks

These books are for Rachel, who approved.

First published in Great Britain in 2000
as a Dolphin paperback
by Orion Children's Books
a division of the Orion Publishing Group Ltd
Orion House
5 Upper St Martin's Lane
London WC2H 9EA

A catalogue record for this book is
available from the British Library.

Typeset at The Spartan Press Ltd,
Lymington, Hants
Printed in Great Britain by
Clays Ltd, St Ives plc

ISBN 1 85881 801 X

One

Cat's always got one over me. She sent this e-mail saying she was dying to see me, signing off with – 'PS I got my nose pierced. It's wicked.' What she meant was that she was dying to show off her nose stud to me so that I could be envious. Which I will be.

Cat is my friend in Cornwall. She stays in the cottage behind us and we're the same age (fourteen). I've seen her every summer since I was one year old, though we don't see each other the rest of the year. I live in London and she lives miles away.

What made the nose stud information harder to bear was the fact that I've also had some metal inserted into my face recently – that must-have fashion item: train tracks on my teeth. I've had a sort of miniature metal coat hanger affair that I wear at night for some time, but this was the big one, a whole year of agony and ugliness to look forward to.

As a list sort of person I had to try and sort out this sorry state of affairs:

Things you can't do with a fixed brace
Eat
Smile
Play the clarinet
Kiss

I thought that ruled out most of my life's essential activities, but then I had to try and squeeze out another list for things you *can* do.

Things you can still do with a fixed brace, maybe
Drink
Dress up
Swim
Sunbathe
Dance
Cuddle
(I won't go on)

So maybe it's not *too* bad. Mind you, several of the above recreations do depend on you being at least half way attractive.

I'm sort of looking forward to seeing Cat down in Cornwall – we have a lot of laughs together. And there are loads of other people that I can't wait to see. But before we go on holiday there's a sleepover here at my friend Holly's house. Holly rang me when I'd just had the brace fitted and it was total agony. I haven't seen her since she got back from a free trip to Barbados with her dad's school, so no doubt I'll feel envious of her too. She has some secret plan she wants to share with me and, unlike Cat, these are friends I feel safe with. (Sounds funny, I know, but Cat's someone who keeps you on your toes. You can't drop your guard.) And I adore sleepovers, especially when we talk for hours and hours about everything.

We had the video and we had the food. Then Holly

made us shut up and listen. Alex never shuts up and listens – she's the tomboy, always telling jokes. But Zoe was curious and so was I. As I said, Holly spent the first half of the summer holidays in Barbados. So she's come home with a deep tan – and a boyfriend! So I am envious, twice over. Holly's never had a real boyfriend before, but she's madly in love with this guy, Jonty. She met a whole crowd of people on the beach who were rich enough to stay in a really posh hotel. Jonty's practically a member of the royal family, and Oliver O'Neill (you know, famous film director?) was there with his two kids, so Holly got to meet them all. But the weird part is, there was another girl at the hotel, called Maddy, and *she's* a friend of a girl I know. Small world!

And that brought us on to the thing Holly wanted to tell us. Maddy and three friends (including Hannah, the one I know) had made a pact that they would all have a holiday romance and then report back afterwards. Apparently Maddy got together with the film director's son in Barbados, and Hannah, who was on a music course with me, certainly had a thing with one of the guys (one of the few decent ones) there. Of course, I'd no idea she was doing it for a dare, it all seemed pretty real to me.

Holly wanted the four of us to do the same thing. All very well for her – she's already snared her man. Zoe won't have any trouble, but Alex hasn't shown much interest in the opposite sex to date, and as for me – well I don't exactly fancy my chances with this thing in my mouth! But Holly was so enthusiastic that I had to say I'd do my best. In fact there are quite a few guys I like in

Cornwall, and it's a dead romantic place, so perhaps it won't be too impossible a task.

There are only two more weeks left of the summer holidays, so the pressure's on. Holly's going to visit Jonty in his stately home but the other two are staying in London. Alex plays a tennis tournament every year, which could be interesting, and Zoe's doing a theatre project, so that could be a rich hunting ground as well. Hmm. Not such a bad idea after all. In fact, I was warming to it – it would be a laugh to hear what the others got up to!

When I got home next morning the car was packed for our trip to Cornwall. My brother Tim was already jammed amongst the beach towels and wetsuits with his Walkman on, nose in a magazine, his hand dipping automatically into a packet of crisps, as if we were already driving down the motorway at eighty miles an hour.

'In you get, Jo-jo,' said my dad, 'and I'll pack the last things around you. I want to be on the road by midday. The thought of that first cool beer by the barbecue at the cottage is what's keeping me going.' Dad shares the cottage with his two sailing-mad brothers and their families. Sometimes we overlap with them, but it's better when we don't because my cousins are small and noisy and can be annoying. My brother Tim is fairly annoying too, but he's only a year and a bit younger than me (and almost taller). He has his own friends in Cornwall and I have Cat, so our paths don't cross that much.

Some people moan about going on holiday with their

families, but I don't mind being with mine. Mum seems to enjoy me being a teenager and we go shopping together – I get most things I want in the way of clothes and make-up. Dad thinks he's dead funny and witty. He shows off to my friends – he likes them to think he's still pretty cool (as *if*) – but he's OK.

My parents are a bit over-protective, I suppose – they took me away from the comprehensive I went to with the others because they thought it was too big and impersonal. It wasn't bad, but I did feel intimidated sometimes, and I do prefer the school I'm at, so perhaps they did the right thing. I've never quite got over not fitting in at the first school. I tried to be like the others. Holly and I both got on fine at first, but somehow Holly made new friends more quickly. She never left me out – we're still really close – I just wasn't as confident as her. Before, it had always been Alex who was the odd one out, being so tall and boyish, but once she and Zoe got together they were cool in their own eccentric way. So Holly didn't miss me when I left – she's very pretty and she'll be popular wherever she is. I got on better at a girls' school – though even there I'm still conscious of the fact that everyone knew each other before I arrived and that I've got a lot of catching up to do. I've got some good friends now, and I've been invited to a few parties, so I shouldn't really worry. Luckily I get to meet people, especially boys, because of other things I do – like playing the clarinet, and going to Cornwall – surfers' paradise.

I think about boys all the time these days. It's terrible! I might be waiting for the bus or walking to my music lesson or just looking out of the car window, and if I see

5

a boy I start to fantasise about him straight away. When I went on this music course earlier in the holidays, I spent half the time wondering which boys might fancy me. I had a big thing about one guy – a drummer. I kept thinking he was looking at me. He even spoke to me once or twice. But in the end he started going out with a really pretty girl who was older than us, so I suppose he hadn't been interested in me at all. I was quite depressed when that happened. I get crushes on guys in films and soaps – I think about them all the time and have little daydreams about meeting them and me being the only girl they really care about. That's partly why having this brace is such a downer – it makes it so much harder to fantasise about being kissed!

Dad threw in the last few bits and pieces. 'Strange to be leaving your clarinet behind,' he said. The brace means I can't play for a year at least, though I'm sure I'll pick it up again. I've already done Grade Seven. I can still play a guitar if there's one to hand.

'Dad? Do we need to bring a guitar or is there one already at the cottage?'

'There's usually a crummy one there,' he said. 'Anyway, there isn't an inch of room left in the car. And it's twelve o'clock, I want to go.'

Dad behaves like a team leader over the journey. He never lets Mum take a turn at driving. We set off with military punctuality. Two and a half hours. Stop at Gordano services. Another two and a half hours and we're there. Lots of travelling time for thinking and wondering how it's going to be. Will I fit in this year? Will people like me? Have I brought the right clothes?

Do I *own* the right clothes? Cornwall holiday fashions are always slightly different from the ones at home – like a darker tan, they set apart the people who've been there for weeks. Surfie stuff – you'd expect that – plus little hippie touches, like bracelets or henna tattoos or hair wraps, and you can't tell exactly what they're going to be until you get down there. In London terms Cat isn't as fashionable as my friends, but in Cornwall she's always got it just right. I wondered what it would be this year. Well, the nose stud for starters. And I'd never be allowed one of those! No, I always have to go for the instant fashions – the ones that can be bought in beach shops.

I thought about the boys I know in Cornwall, surprise, surprise. If I'm honest, it's not many. I made a mental list. It went like this:

The boy at the bike hire place who I used to think was cool.
A couple of guys Cat and I used to see on the beach most days.
The kids I see every year, of course – Archie and Harry, whose dad sails with my uncle.
Tanya-down-the-lane's older brother, Ivan.
Seth who lives at the top and isn't happy unless he's standing on a board of some kind.
All the boys who camp in the garden of Liza's house. They're friends of Liza's older sister Ellie, and a bit too old for us. (Ellie's boyfriend last year was gorgeous.)

And each year there's an older kids' scene that starts in

the pub, but I wasn't part of it last summer. *This year it will be different*, I thought. I will simply make it my business to get to know people. And have a holiday romance, of course.

'Fifty pence to the first one to see the sea!' my dad said.

Already! And there it was. 'I can see it!' Tim and I both yelled, as we always do.

'You'll have to have fifty pence each, then,' said my dad, as he always does. Twenty minutes of winding, high-sided lanes with leaning, windswept trees later we were there. 'Tredunnet', it said on the gate, and we piled out of the car and made our way up the long front path to the low doorway where my Uncle Alan and Aunt Pat and two small cousins – plus their big white labrador – were waiting for us, blue smoke already curling up from the barbecue, cold beer for Dad and Mum at the ready.

Two

The cottage is brilliant. I absolutely love it. I knew which room I wanted and I was desperate to bag it. 'Which rooms are ours?' I asked my uncle. My parents were already ensconced by the barbecue. They said the unloading could wait.

'We're in the yellow room and the boys are in the bunk beds next door. We thought Tim might like to join them.'

'Please can I have the blue room?' I asked, trying not to make it sound too desirable. If I was Tim, I'd definitely want it.

'Go ahead,' said the adults, wanting to get back to their conversation.

'Tim?'

'I don't care,' he said, miraculously. 'I'll go in the bunks – or downstairs if I don't like it.'

Great! I hauled my bag upstairs and made myself at home. The blue room is the smallest room in the cottage. It's over the front door and it has a deep window-seat where you can sit and watch over the front garden and the lane beyond. The cushion in the window-seat is covered with the same blue-striped material that the curtains are made of. There's a little hanging wardrobe in the corner, also blue-striped, and a pretty chair and chest of drawers. It's perfect. I always used to have to go in the bunks with my brother and cousins. The blue room was usually set aside for an elderly relation, but we didn't have any with us this time.

I unpacked my clothes and put them away in the drawers and the hanging wardrobe. It made me feel as though I was staying. I pulled out my Discman (birthday present) and my favourite CDs and set them up on the bedside table. My make-up went on top of the chest of drawers. Then my drawing things – I always have a sketchpad with me – in the window-seat. And then Monk. Down the bed. Monk, I'm afraid, is my oldest soft toy, a monkey (you guessed). He's been quite a comfort to me recently, with my mouth hurting so much. Anyway, no excuses. I'm sentimental about him and he comes everywhere with me. It was odd not to be unpacking my clarinet for a quick toot. It might seem a bit tragic practising a musical instrument on holiday, but I just say it's not tragic if you enjoy it. I must remember to dig out the crummy guitar, though Dad's bound to find it if I don't.

I opened the window and waved to the others down in the garden.

'Do you want a burger?' my aunt called up.

'You might as well,' said my mum, 'because I'm not cooking again later.'

I looked back at my little room, heard the seagulls calling and the sheep bleating in the field at the back. It would keep. 'OK! I'm coming down.'

It was so great to be here again. Tim was rolling around on the grass with the two cousins and the dog. As soon as I'd eaten my burger I joined in.

'Hi! Hi there, Josie!' It was Cat. She appeared at the side gate. It was nearest to their cottage which is behind ours. I stopped mid-roll and sat up, squinting into the sun. I already had grass stains on my trousers.

Cat looks like a cat. She has dark hair, short at the moment and still wet from swimming, though I detected some coloured streaks in there. Her green eyes slant upwards at the sides, accentuated by her good cheekbones. And of course there was the nose stud, twinkling. Cat wore a bikini top with shorts and flip-flops. I took in the extras, logged them so that I could replicate them as quickly as possible: a henna tattoo round the top of her arm; a leather thong with a square of tiny beads on it round her neck; a plaited leather bracelet; amazing nail varnish on her fingernails and toenails.

'Hi, Cat.'

She came over. 'Wow, Josie, you've got train tracks!'

As if I hadn't noticed them myself. 'The nose stud is cool,' I said.

'There's a shop in Newquay where you can get it done,' she said.

I looked over to Dad, but he was making throat-slitting gestures. 'My parents might take some persuading,' I said. Cat and I usually settle in for a long gossip as soon as we meet up. I wanted to know exactly what was what and who was who. 'Have you got time to talk?' I asked.

'Of course,' said Cat, 'but I'm going down to the pub later. Do you want to come?'

'I don't know,' I said. 'Don't know if I'll be allowed.'

'But you're on holiday,' said Cat. 'Surely you'll be allowed? That's where everybody goes.'

I could practically see my dad's ears flapping. He was listening in disapprovingly. 'Let's go to your house,' I said. 'I want you to do my nails.'

'So when will we see you?' asked Dad, still wanting to keep tabs on me.

'I don't know,' I said, wishing he'd back off.

'Well, I'm going out in an hour,' said Cat.

'In an hour!' I said, and followed her.

Cat's cottage is almost directly behind ours in the jumble of buildings that make up the old part of the village. New and quite ugly houses line the road to the sea, but back here it's surrounded by fields and still pretty. I wouldn't want to be anywhere else, though I suppose the best place would be right down by the beach and the sailing club, so you could walk everywhere. That's where the pub is.

I followed Cat into her kitchen. Her parents were out the back, sipping gin and tonic and reading the papers. They're older than mine and seem vaguely amused by their only daughter. Cat gets away with murder. They probably think the nose stud is a hoot. Cat helped herself to a couple of cans of Coke from the fridge and offered one of them to me. We sat down. 'I want you to come to the pub because I want you to meet my boyfriend,' she said, watching my face for a reaction.

'Cat!' I squealed. 'Why didn't you say?' This would change things a bit. 'Come on, who is he? Tell me all about him.'

'He's one of the crowd down the pub. A windsurfer. There's a whole group of them. Gorgeous hunky blokes.'

'What's he called? What does he look like?'

'Big. Hunky. Windsurfery.'

'Was he here last year? Might I have seen him?'

'I don't think he was. I'd never seen him before. He's called Matt.'

'More! Tell me more! What colour's his hair? Is he cute or is he hard? Was it love at first sight?'

'Josie! It's not that big a deal.'

'But it is! My friend Holly's just started going out with a guy and she's madly in love with him and it's just so exciting! She can't stop talking about him.'

'OK. Well, he looks kind of cute but he acts hard. He's got dark hair and a good body.'

'Is he sexy? Is he a good kisser?'

'Oh come on, Josie. Give me a break. I'm not going to tell you everything.'

I was stung. 'You always have until now.'

'Well. This is different. More grown-up.'

'Oh. All right.' I felt hurt. This was meant to be the fun part, wasn't it? Talking about boys with your girl friends? But I tried to swallow my disappointment. I didn't want Cat to think I was some silly little innocent. 'Huh, say no more, Cat. I get your meaning. Now tell me about everyone else while you do my nails.'

We went up to her room – a beautiful attic that ran across the top of their cottage. You could see the sea from here. She sat me on her bed and brought over loads of little bottles. She shook them vigorously one by one. 'Feet first.'

'Harry and Archie? Tanya and Ivan? Seth? Liza and Ellie?'

'Harry, Archie and Ivan are all juvenile and I don't see them.' (So that was half my entire list of boys ruled out.) 'Tanya's broken her ankle and her leg's in a plaster cast, so she hasn't been much fun. Liza goes around with her. But it's worth staying in with Liza because of all Ellie's friends camping in their garden. D'you know there are about fifteen of them – mostly guys?'

'What about Seth? You forgot him.'

'Never knowingly not on a board. He goes all the way down to the beach on his skateboard. Ever so dangerous when there's traffic around. Then he spends all day on a surfboard and hitches a ride back!'

'Good old Seth. Does he look the same?'

'Got dreads this year. Oh, and train tracks like you, poor guy!' Cat had finished my toenails. They were a work of art. 'Hands,' she commanded, and set to painting my fingernails.

'What are you wearing to the pub?' If I could persuade my parents to let me go I wanted to turn up looking right.

'Nothing special. You know, trousers, top.'

Cat's hair had dried. 'Hey Cat, you've got colours in your hair.'

'Good, aren't they? D'you want me to do yours?'

I thought about it. Dad's protective of his darling daughter but he's learning to be indulgent. He's used to make-up and nail varnish but he hated it when I had my ears pierced. He might react badly to coloured streaks in my fair hair. Mum wouldn't mind at all, but I wanted them to let me go down to the pub, so I thought I'd better go easy. 'Tomorrow. Tonight I'm pleading for a late pass and I don't want to frighten my dad.'

'Make him say yes. I really want to know what you think of Matt. I'm cycling down in about ten minutes. See you there!'

'Oh there you are,' said Mum. 'We were about to set off for our traditional first night walk along the dunes to say hello to the sea. You're just in time.'

'I was about to change, Mum. Cat wants me to go to the pub near the sailing club.'

'The pub? I'm not having my fourteen-year-old daughter going to the pub!' thundered Dad, coming down the stairs.

In fact my uncle came to my rescue. 'Oh all the kids go there, Jim. They stand outside in a great heaving mass with their Cokes. Josie'll be perfectly safe.'

'And how do you intend getting there?' asked my dad, determined not to be mollified too easily.

I hadn't thought of that. 'I suppose I hoped you'd give me a lift. I'd like to hire a bike at some point, and then I wouldn't be so dependent on you.'

'And get yourself killed by some idiot coming too fast round a bend? Not likely.'

'We'll wait for you to change, love,' said Mum, the pacifier. 'Come down with us and we'll drop you off.'

'But I thought we were all going for a walk,' said Dad. 'I wanted Josie to be with us.' He wasn't going to make it easy.

'I'll come for the walk,' I said, sensing that I was going to have to work at this, but that it would be worth it in the end. 'And then, perhaps, I could go to the pub with Cat for a bit, and then ring you and you could come and fetch me.'

'Oh, taxi service is it now?' said Dad, but he was coming round.

'I just thought you'd prefer me not to be home too late,' I said sweetly, and knew I'd won.

I changed into my Kookaï trousers and top and slapped on a bit of make-up, though nothing seems to detract from the metal on my teeth. Sometimes I can hardly bear even to see myself in the mirror. I bunged a sweatshirt and my purse into a bag. I didn't know if I was wearing the right things or not. I swapped my sandals for my new trainers, a label no one can quarrel with, and went out to join my family.

We passed the pub on the drive down to the car park by the dunes. People were already spilling out across the road. None of them looked very old. I couldn't see Cat amongst them, but it didn't matter until I got back from our walk.

The dunes are lovely. When you've climbed up above the beach you can just let go and sprint with the wind in your hair along tiny sandy footpaths up and down the tussocky little hills. Mum and Dad walked along arm in arm while Tim and I chased each other all over the place. It was a beautiful evening – plenty of people were still in the water, paddling, rockpooling, windsurfing, sailing. Idyllic. It was great to be back.

I said I'd walk from the car park. I'd be fine as long as I had the mobile. But Dad insisted on coming with me. In the end it was go with him or don't go at all. He even put his arm round my shoulders, and I didn't dare shake him off – partly because I didn't want him to change his mind and partly because I didn't want to hurt him.

And there was Cat. She was cuddled up to a guy who I assumed must be Matt and she had a drink in one hand and a cigarette in the other – as did all the people around her. They were sitting on a low wall on the opposite side of the road from the pub. I spotted Tanya with her plaster not far away and Liza and Ellie. I couldn't wait to join them. 'OK, Dad? I've got the mobile.' I wanted to lose him before he took in what my friends were up to and changed his mind.

'Not so fast young lady.' Aagh. 'I want to find someone sensible to leave you with.' He peered into the gloomy interior of the pub. 'Good, I thought so, there's David.' (David is Archie and Harry's dad.) 'David? David!' he called, and David came blinking out into the road. 'I'm leaving Josie here for a while. Could you keep an eye on her? Thanks so much.' He turned to me. 'There, you'll be fine,' he said, and set off in the direction of the car park.

I wanted to die, but it wasn't over yet. 'Hello, Josie,' said David jovially. He has a loud booming voice, good for yelling instructions to his crew. 'Can I get you a squash or something?'

'I – I'm with some friends, thank you David,' I said. 'Over there.'

'Oh, jolly good, jolly good,' said David. 'Over there, did you say? Just so I can do my duty by your old dad. Fine.'

I crawled over to Cat and her group. 'Oh great,' said Cat. 'That's all I need, Harry and Archie's dad watching my every move.'

'Sorry,' I said. 'I don't really think he'll be looking in this direction, though, not if he's drinking inside.'

Liza and Tanya were more sympathetic. 'Parents!' said Tanya. 'Mine expect me to do everything with Ivan. It would be easier if Ivan had a few bad habits!'

'Mine have given up,' said Liza, laughing. 'With a houseful of Ellie's friends you have to! The lads are shameless. They're nice though. Mum adores them – twelve boys as well as three of Ellie's friends from school.'

Cat had calmed down. 'Hey, Josie,' she said. 'This is Matt.' Matt nodded in my direction but carried on talking to his group of boys. He was so-o-o good-looking. It was obvious that he was very popular. I felt envious of Cat all over again. I was going to have to work extra hard with this brace blighting my features.

'Does anyone want a drink?' I said, thinking that I

couldn't start soon enough, as well as needing one for myself. I had twenty pounds of assorted savings and holiday money in my purse. That got Matt's attention all right!

'I'll go to the bar for you if you like,' he said kindly, holding his hand out for the money. 'They know me there. They think I'm eighteen. What are you having – Josie, is it?'

He knew my name! 'Ooh . . .' I remembered not to smile too broadly in case I put him off and tried to think sophisticated. 'I'll have an Archers please. Thank you.' And he was off into the crowd.

'That was really nice of you,' said Cat, and I glowed, feeling forgiven.

Matt came back with a huge tray of pint glasses. He handed me my little glass and bottle of Archers. Cat was having the same. 'No change I'm afraid,' he said. 'In fact, you owe me thirty pence.'

'I'm sorry,' I said, and delved into my purse. I probably had thirty pence in coppers. I put my drink on the wall and started counting out my change, though Matt seemed to have forgotten as he handed round the beers. I offered it to Cat. 'Here, you give it to him.' Cat took it and I sipped at my drink. Liza and Tanya had moved away to join a swirling group of slightly older kids – Ellie and the campers. They had a raucous game going that looked fun, but I felt pretty cool being with Matt and co.

I looked around. Leaning against the front of the pub near the door, slightly separate from any other group, were two more guys, who seemed to be gazing out over our heads towards the boats on the estuary. I don't know why I hadn't noticed them straight away, because if I'd been listing people in order of charisma (might try that later on) I could have been tempted to put them above even Matt and the rest of our lot. I watched them when no one was talking to me. They both had sunbleached hair and tanned faces and limbs, wore long shorts and T-shirts like all the other boys. They looked very easy in themselves, as if they were very old friends, maybe related. Everyone stopped to say something to them on their way in and out of the pub. I decided to go to the loo so I could get a closer look.

One of them was probably about eighteen, the other more like fifteen. They weren't saying anything when I went past, just two pairs of sea-grey eyes looking out to sea. They were both wearing leather bracelets, each with a tiny carved dolphin knotted in. I determined to find out more about the dolphin boys (as I'd already christened them), but when I came out of the pub again David was right in the doorway beside them and booming, 'Gracious, Josie. I'd almost forgotten you. How terrible of me! Would you like a lift up now or is your father coming to fetch you?' The younger boy caught my eye. I thought he looked sympathetic at first, but then I realised he must despise someone so pathetically controlled by their parents.

I kept my eyes on David. 'I'm fine, thank you, David. I've got the mobile to ring Dad when I'm ready.'

'Oh very sensible. I'll call in at Tredunnet to tell him I'm back but you're still at large. Don't want to neglect my duty. See you soon, dear. Harry and Archie are looking forward to seeing you too.'

I dived out and went back to my group, who somehow

all seemed to have another drink. Cat was handing round cigarettes. 'Go on, Josie,' she said. 'You've got to have some vices.'

I saw David driving off, so although I don't smoke really I thought this would be a good chance to up my street cred. 'Don't mind if I do,' I said, and took one.

'There,' said Cat. 'This is just so cool, don't you think? Everyone's here. It's like a big party every night. So who do you fancy?' She nudged me. 'I think Paul over there is cute – not as cute as Matt, but I know he hasn't got a girlfriend.' I looked at Paul. I could see straight away why he hadn't got a girlfriend, but I didn't say that to Cat. The nicotine was going to my head and my knees. Matt was starting to grope Cat and I was beginning to feel like a gooseberry, too tired to chat up anyone, let alone hunky guys.

It was nearly dark. A pair of headlights drilled into the crowd, who were pressed against the edges of the road as a car pushed its way through. 'Oy!' shouted Matt, thumping the roof as the car edged past. Everyone laughed.

Except me. The window slid down and my dad stuck his head out. 'Anyone seen Josie Liddell?' he asked the world in general. I stamped out my cigarette and jumped in, if only to put an end to my embarrassment. I knew of course that the road was a dead end because of the sea, and the only way back was through the crowd again.

'Did you have a nice time, dear?' said my mother from the sofa as Dad and I ducked in through the low front door. No sign of Tim or my young cousins.

I said, 'Fine thanks. I'm off to bed,' and shot upstairs to the haven of the little blue room. I wasn't going to mention a round of drinks costing twenty pounds. I just hoped it had bought me a bit of popularity. I sat up in bed with my sketch book and did a drawing of the dolphin boys – I just had to – along with a few frames of dolphins morphing into humans. Then a list of the people I'd seen already:

Have seen
Cat
Matt – Cat's gorgeous boyfriend. Everyone seems to look up to him.
The dolphin boys: two cool guys, v brown, blond, sort of Viking looks. Don't know who they are, but everyone seems to know them.
Matt's friends: Luke, Paul and Sebastian. I just about got them sorted out. Paul was one of the ones on his own.
Tanya (leg in plaster), Liza, Ellie.
Ellie's friends – recognised some of the boys vaguely.

Haven't seen
Harry and Archie, Ivan or Seth. Looking forward to seeing Seth with dreads and a BRACE like mine!

Three

I slept in quite late. Surprising considering how bright the sunlight was and the noise my cousins were making. I lay there dozing awhile, listening to the seagulls, savouring the fact that I was in Cornwall in the blue room and that it was a sunny day. And that I'd slept right through the night without being woken by the pain of the train tracks.

I heard a strange gushing sound going down the side of the house and continuing down the lane towards the sea. It took me a few moments to work out that it must be Seth on his skateboard. I leapt over to my window, but I was too late. Seth with dreads and brace, carrying a surfboard and riding a skateboard would have been quite a sight! 'Outta sight,' he would have said.

I was up now, so I shambled downstairs in my pyjamas. Tim was eating breakfast on his own. I could hear the rest of the family dispersed around the house. Tim grunted at me. 'What was the pub like?'

'Cool,' I said, putting aside the hideous memory of the twenty pounds.

'Waste of money,' said Tim, as if he'd read my mind. 'Stick around with Mum and Dad – they'll buy you a drink.'

'Not the point, Tim. It's the company you go for. I only had one drink.'

'Bet it was that nasty sticky stuff.'

'None of your business.'

He sniffed my hair. 'Bet you were smoking.'

'All pubs smell of smoke Tim. Anyway, what's got into you?'

'Dunno. I just haven't met up with any of my friends yet.'

'You will, as soon as you get down to the beach. You always do.' Tim does all the Cornwall things, like sailing and windsurfing and proper stand-up surfing. Dad often says he should have been one of my uncles' sons. Dad was the least sporty one in the family, more into music than watersports. He'll go out in a boat, but he doesn't own one. One of the reasons we come to the cottage when we do is to coincide with a music festival in a little church a few miles away. It's one of those bizarre tiny festivals that attracts really big names. Some years they run a scratch orchestra and choir for kids. You have to be good, but you get to sing or play under a famous conductor. I don't talk about it to Cat and the others – people have funny ideas about classical music. Anyway, this year I can't play because of my brace, so perhaps that's better all round.

Mum and my aunt came into the kitchen together. 'Beach picnic at the bay today,' said Mum. 'Is that OK with you two?'

'Of course it is,' I said. 'It wouldn't be our Cornwall holiday without at least three picnics down there.'

'When's Uncle Alan going down to the beach?' Tim asked my aunt.

'I'm sure he'd take you and the boys down this morning,' she said. 'It would give me a break.'

'Can we go shopping this morning, Mum?' I asked. 'Just one of the beach shops.'

'Is that OK, Pat?' Mum asked my aunt.

'That'll make it a real break!'

'You're on, Josie. Get dressed quickly.'

I called in on Cat before we left, but there was no one about. Mum drove me to the beach shop. We parked and walked over the beach we call the surfing beach. The shop sells and hires out surf gear, but it has a whole floor of other stuff. Mum enjoys it as much as I do. 'It doesn't change much from year to year, does it?' she said. 'Look, here's the little dress we bought you last year. And they've still got these trousers.' Surfing fashion labels have really silly names, like Kangaroo Poo and Rip Curl and Sex Wax.

'Oooh, this is gorgeous. Can I try it on Mum?' I'd fallen for a little top. It was just the right size and Mum agreed to buy it for me.

As we were waiting to pay I rummaged around in the baskets on the counter. They were full of small things – hats, sunglasses, bracelets. One of them had the knotted leather jewellery Cat was wearing. I found some with tiny bead squares, just like hers, but I didn't want to get something identical. And then I found a single bracelet with a tiny carved wooden dolphin knotted into it. I knew exactly where I'd seen it before. It was beautiful. 'Last one, that is,' said the shopkeeper in her Cornish accent. 'I tried to order more, but they said they were turning out too costly to produce.'

'Could I have it, Mum?'

'Well, I'm paying for the clothes – don't you have your own money for that, darling?'

'I've left my purse behind,' I mumbled.

'Oh well, I haven't handed over my plastic yet,' she said. 'Can you add the bracelet on? And then you can pay me back, love. It's only one pound fifty.'

As we left the shop I could have sworn I caught sight of one of my dolphin boys amongst the hanging wet-suits, but I suspect it was an illusion.

Cat was home when we got back. She asked me if I wanted to come over after our picnic so she could put the colours in my hair. Great!

We always go to the bay for picnics. It doesn't change. It's a great curve of beach with rocky coves all round. The waves are very gentle because the sea here is still part of the estuary. You get a few windsurfers, but mostly it's little kids paddling and building sandcastles. Alan arrived a bit after us with Tim and the boys. They'd been sailing with Archie and Harry, who came along too. It was the first time I'd seen them this holiday. We've grown up with them. Archie's a bit younger than me and Harry's a bit older. They're kind of dorky, but nice.

'Heard about Cat and Matt?' said Harry, as we chucked pebbles into the sea. He hadn't said a word about my brace.

'I met him last night in the pub,' I said.

'Oh yeah, Dad said you were down there. I know those guys from windsurfing. I think Matt's a bit of a show-off, myself.'

(Dear old Harry.) 'Cat seems to like him.'

'I suppose girls would find him quite good-looking.'

'And he probably finds Cat quite good-looking!'

'Yeah.' Harry's always been a bit in love with Cat.

Two windsurfers were sailing across the bay. They were very close to the shore. Harry and I stopped hurling pebbles to watch them.

'They're good,' said Harry.

I recognised them! 'Hey, Harry! Do you know who they are?'

'Don't think so!' said Harry. He peered after my dolphin boys, but they'd vanished behind the rocks.

Mum was calling. 'Josie, do you want to go and get ice-creams for everyone? The shop at the top's open.'

'I'll come with you,' said Harry, when Mum had given me the money.

I took everyone's orders. There were twelve of us. Harry and I would have to make two journeys. As we did the last shift Harry said, 'Why didn't you have one yourself, Josie?'

'I'd rather have the money,' I told him. 'Don't tell anyone, please. I've eaten it, OK?'

Liza and Tanya were already in Cat's bedroom when I arrived. 'This is going to be wicked,' said Cat. 'Colours look great in fair hair.'

'It didn't work on me,' said Liza. She's got very thick, bushy hair, mid-brown.

'It would probably work on me,' said Tanya, 'but I'm not letting you near it!' Her hair's about the same colour as mine. 'I feel distinctive enough hobbling along with this thing on my leg.'

'I feel *distinctive*,' I said, 'with these horrendous train tracks. I just want to divert people's attention from them.'

'I think they're quite attractive,' said Liza.

'Huh!'

'No, really. They're sort of twinkly. And you've got a nice mouth. They draw attention to that. You ought to wear lots of lip gloss.'

'Thanks, Liza. That makes me feet a bit less awful about them.'

'And you get them on the National Health,' Liza went on. 'Cheaper than a nose stud, eh, Cat?'

Cat laughed. 'But not so cool.'

'No, you're right,' said Liza. 'I want to get my eyebrow pierced but my parents won't let me.'

'Just do it,' said Cat. 'Then it's too late to stop you.'

'My mum would hit the roof if I got my nose pierced,' said Tanya. 'She did when Ivan got an earring. About the only cool thing Ivan's ever done.'

'I haven't seen him this year,' I said. 'Where is he?'

'Where every sensible person goes when they come to the seaside – in a church, playing his violin!' said Tanya, and the others all screeched with laughter. I didn't say anything. As I said, I keep quiet about my musical activities with this lot. I'd forgotten Ivan was a musician. He probably hadn't been a high enough standard before.

'Come on,' said Cat. 'Strip off, Josie. Let's do your hair.'

'Keep it subtle,' I said.

'Trust me,' said Cat.

Half an hour later I regarded myself in the mirror.

'What do you think?' said Liza. 'I think it looks great. Really pretty.'

'Not bad,' said Tanya. 'It makes you look interesting.'

'Thanks!'

'No! An interesting person. A bit hippie-ish.'

'Exactly,' said Cat. 'It'll go down a storm in the pub. Matt has this thing about girls who colour their hair. He thinks it's dead sexy.'

'I'm not out to get Matt, am I?' I said, secretly pleased to know I might get his attention. 'He's bagged.'

'I'm supposed to like Luke,' said Liza, 'but I'm not sure yet.'

'And I quite like Sebastian,' said Tanya. 'Though I don't expect he likes me.'

'Oh don't be so Eeyoreish, Tanya,' said Cat. 'I'm sure he does, and he's better looking than Paul.'

The one she'd reserved for me. I didn't remind her of it. 'Are you all coming tonight?' she asked.

'I don't have a lot of money,' was my answer. 'I might have enough by tomorrow night though.'

'Depends,' said Liza. 'If I just stick with Ellie I might. But her friends are so noisy, it's embarrassing. They were playing these silly pub games last night. I really wanted to disown them.'

'They just looked as if they were having fun, to me,' I said.

'I'd have been embarrassed if it had been my sister,' said Tanya.

'But you went over to join in last night, didn't you?' I said.

'Sort of,' said Liza. 'I had to find someone to drive me back. I had to be home by half past ten.'

So I wasn't the only one with a curfew.

'What about you, Tanya?'

'I need a lift too.'

'If getting there is the only problem,' said Cat, 'I'll get

one of my parents to drive us all down. Please come, Josie.'

'I haven't got the money, Cat.' I thought she'd realise why, but she obviously didn't.

'Can I make you all up, now?' said Cat. 'And I can do nails, too. Show them yours, Josie.'

We had such a cool afternoon, mucking about with clothes and make-up. I nipped back to the cottage to get my new things to show everybody. I do like being just girls together. I was glad Cat wasn't spending all her time with Matt.

'What were you lot doing this morning?' I asked. 'I called round here, Cat, but you weren't in.'

'We were on the beach,' said Tanya, 'weren't we, Liza? Where were you, Cat?'

'Oh – I – got home pretty late. I was probably still asleep.'

I went back to our cottage for supper. I thought about going to the pub and buying an orange squash or something with the 90p I'd saved on the ice-cream, but I couldn't really face having to persuade my parents all over again. Although Mum really liked my hair, Dad wasn't so sure. I told him it washed out (I didn't tell him how many washes it would take) and he said he might get used to it. Then Seth called in on his way home from the beach. We were all sitting in the garden still, digesting treacle tart and clotted cream, one of our holiday specials from the local delicatessen.

'Yo, dudes!' he called. You have to see Seth, he's a complete one-off. He has gingerish hair which he wears in dreadlocks with extensions, all tied back in a ponytail. He's my age, but about ten feet tall. With a mouth full of metal. He goes everywhere on a skateboard. Right now he was carrying both a surfboard and a skateboard. Needless to say, he's a great snowboarding person in winter. He's a big old hippie, really.

My mum has a soft spot for Seth. 'Yo, Seth!' she called, embarrassingly. 'There's some treacle tart going begging if you fancy a bit.'

'I always fancy a bit, Mrs L,' said Seth, loping up the path. 'Hey, Jo-jo – like the stripy hair, and the metal-work.'

'Yours isn't so bad, either,' I said.

'Bummer, isn't it?' he said.

'Yup. But temporary. Think how beautiful we're going to be.'

'You, yes. Me – I don't think so.'

'Well I think you're both quite beautiful as it is,' said Mum. *Do shut up, Mum, ple-hease.* (She's been at the wine.)

Seth simply beamed at Mum and redirected his charm at Tim. 'Yo, Tim. How's it going?'

'All the better for seeing you, mate,' said Tim. Seth has this effect on people.

Seth turned back to me. 'Fancy a little twang later on?' he asked. 'I've done a couple of songs. Just waiting for you.' Seth writes grungey songs. Every now and then he persuades me to sing along with him.

'Do we know where the crummy guitar is yet, Dad?'

'I've put it in your room,' he said.

'OK, Seth. When?'

'Come over eightish?'

*

So that's what I did while the others went to the pub, and I couldn't help feeling I was missing out. Seth's cottage is right at the top. His family is totally laid back and happy. They spend all summer here – I don't know what they do the rest of the year. Actually I think his dad teaches art somewhere, or CDT or something. His mum bakes bread, does crystal readings and raises a whole tribe of little Seths. Their cottage is full of patchwork and barefoot toddlers and nappies and the garden is full of strange herbs.

Seth's songs weren't bad – they were all about waiting for some girl to come home and longing to see her face again. Etc, etc. Fairly standard words, but the music was pretty interesting.

'You're getting better, Seth.'

'Hey!'

'No, I mean it. I quite enjoy singing this one, and the chords make sense for a change.'

'That's because I've been practising.'

'Good man.'

Seth made some drinks and we took them outside. I tried to sound him out about the guys Cat had met. I told him I thought Matt was really cool.

'Yeah, he's cool,' said Seth. 'They're pretty cool. Top surfers too. Matt's been in Portugal most of the summer. Bit keen on himself.'

'So what do you think of him and Cat?'

'What's to think?'

'Cat's my best friend. Is he nice enough for her?'

'Don't ask me questions like that, Jo-jo. And don't ask Harry! He's gutted.'

'Poor old Harry.'

*

Cat's car drew up as I made my way home at about eleven. She didn't see me. They dropped Tanya off, and as she was hobbling down her garden path I heard Cat's dad having a go. 'I don't care, Catherine. We were worried sick about you last night, and I'm not having it happen again.' And then a door slammed. Perhaps Cat's parents don't always find her amusing.

In bed I drew some pictures of my leather bracelet with the little dolphin and wrote down some of the words from Seth's song:

> *Hey, Mama, where you bin?*
> *So long and I ain't seen*
> *you-hoo-hoo.*
> *And I missed your smile*
> *And I missed your guile*
> *And I missed your sweet, soft*
> *eye-heye-heyes.*

And so on. Cute, hey?

Things I want to do while I'm here
Find out about the two mystery boys.
Get in with Cat's crowd – on the beach if I can't make it to the pub. (Matt's so gorgeous and I think he quite liked me.)
Not spend too much time with Seth, Harry etc. As Cat said, they're a bit juvenile.
Water ski-ing.
Body-boarding.
Try standing again – Seth started teaching me last year.

Maybe one of Matt's crowd would teach me, or perhaps I should even get proper surfing lessons.

Get a tan.

Go for a bike ride.

Four

Cat came bounding into my bedroom. 'Wakey, wakey! We're going to the surfing beach. You're coming in our car with me and Liza and Tanya and your family are coming down later. Get up!'

'Thanks for asking me what *I* want to do.'

'You want to come to the beach with us, you know you do. It's a lovely day.'

'I suppose so. Now go away and let me get up in private. I'm not at my best in the mornings.' I could see Cat heading for my sketchbook on the windowsill and I didn't want her to look inside. 'Go on, out!'

Cat laughed and went downstairs. 'You'll make sure she comes, won't you?' she asked my dad.

'Of course,' said Dad. 'Can't have anyone wasting a day like this. See you later on the beach, Cat.'

I hadn't realised quite how late it was. Mum had gone shopping with the others, leaving Dad behind. I grabbed a bit of toast and packed a beach bag. 'Should I take one of our boards, Dad?'

'Leave them for us to bring later. You can hire one if you're desperate.' He dug into his pocket. 'Here's a fiver for a board and an ice-cream or whatever. Go on, off you go. I know Cat's waiting – she's acting as though she has some secret assignation down there.'

'Bound to have. See you, Dad!' A whole fiver. Great. I could pay Mum back for the bracelet and still have money for the pub.

Cat's father dropped us off at the surfing beach and we followed her to a place by the rocks where Matt and Sebastian were dug in. Luke and Paul were making their way down to the water. The boys were wearing boardies – none of your fancy stuff. Matt and Sebastian had baseball caps and shades. We laid out our towels beside them and stripped off to our bikinis. I wondered if Matt would notice the colours in my hair. I thought I caught him registering me in my bikini as I put on the suntan lotion, but he and Sebastian were deep in conversation. I lay on my front to read my book and slipped my straps down. I thought I caught him looking at me then, too. It made me feel kind of sexy.

Cat and Liza finally got the boys talking. Soon they were mucking about, chasing each other round. Tanya grumbled to me, 'Liza's supposed to like Luke, but Sebastian likes her better than me. It's not fair. I can hardly walk, let alone run.'

'How was it at the pub last night?' I asked her, hoping for a bit of background to Cat's row with her parents.

'The pub was fine. Packed. Everyone was there. Just that Cat had gone back to Matt's tent with him the night before, and didn't get home till really late – small hours – and her parents were worried, so they came and got her. Matt's dead sexy, isn't he? And now I suppose

Liza will get off with Sebastian and I won't have anyone to be with. I knew this leg would ruin my holiday.'

'I'll be with you, Tanya.'

'You'll probably get off with Luke and I'll be left with the dreaded Paul.'

The others came racing back. Matt and Sebastian were laughing and gasping for breath. Liza was kicking sand at Sebastian. 'Who's coming in the water?' Cat asked. 'The sea's a bit flat, but it's OK for body-boarding.'

'Sebastian said he'd give me a bit of coaching,' said Liza.

'What did I tell you?' Tanya said to me.

'What about you two?' said Cat. 'Are you going to hire boards?'

'I'm not going anywhere,' said Tanya.

I was dying to go in the sea. I thought about hiring a board and then I thought about the money I could save if I didn't. I thought about being a good friend to Tanya last of all.

'I'll stay with Tanya,' I said nobly. Perhaps Matt and Sebastian would be impressed by my sympathetic nature. Anything, *anything* to make them notice me and like me.

'OK,' said Cat, lightly, and the four of them ran down to the waves.

'Now Sebastian will think I'm just someone who people are kind to,' said Tanya gloomily.

Honestly, some people are never satisfied.

Cat and Liza came back first. Liza went off with Tanya to find a loo and I was left with Cat. 'Oh wow, that was so brilliant,' she said.

'Could I have a quick go with your board?' I asked.

'Oh, I suppose so,' she said, smiling up at Matt who was sitting down beside her. They were both glistening with oil and water. They looked very sexy together.

'Damn,' said Matt, feeling in the pocket of his shirt. He held up a lighter and looked mournful.

'What's the matter?' asked Cat.

'I've run out of cigarettes and I haven't got enough money to get any more. I'll have to go to a bank later on.'

'Oh, I need cigarettes,' I said airily. 'I'll nip over and get some. What do you smoke?'

Matt and Cat touched foreheads, sharing a secret giggle. 'Marlboro would be fine.'

I went over to the shop and bought twenty Marlboro. I tried to speak without opening my mouth too wide and no one asked me if I was over sixteen. I didn't get much change from my fiver.

'Hey, cool,' said Matt when I got back. 'Thanks, Josie.' I loved the way he said my name. He lit a cigarette and hung on to the pack.

I picked up Cat's board and went to find some waves. I needed the sea. I suppose it had been worth buying the cigarettes. I wanted Matt to like me, didn't I? I thought of the way his mouth had looked when he said the 'o' in 'Josie'. I wished I could kiss him like Cat did. I wondered what else they did together and then wished I hadn't. The very thought made me feel weak. I ran into the water. Soon I'd have a boyfriend of my own. It couldn't be long – I was making new friends fast.

'That was really sweet of you,' said Cat a bit later, when

we were on our own for a while. 'Matt thinks you're great.'

'No problem,' I said.

'I'm so lucky,' she said with a sigh, and rolled over onto her stomach on the towel next to me. 'Matt wants me to go back to his tent with him again tonight. You'll come down to the pub this time, won't you? Please say you will – my parents won't let me go on my own any more. They think the boys are a bad influence.'

'So you'll go off with Matt and be back by eleven?'

'That's right.'

'What do you do?'

'Josie! Well, we go to his tent, and—' she looked at me slyly. 'Hey! I'm not telling you! Use your imagination!' She sat up to avoid more questions. Not that she'd given me any answers. It was lunchtime and there was a general movement of people leaving to find food and arriving with picnics. Loads of kids seemed to know Cat this year. They said Hi as they went past, or asked where Matt was. It must be brilliant going out with someone so popular.

I saw a large group of people coming in our direction. I heard David's booming voice before I realised that it was our Tredunnet lot and Harry and Archie and their dad. (Their mum stays behind usually. She obviously appreci-ates having a bit of peace and quiet.) 'Here comes my lunch,' I said.

Tanya and Liza appeared behind us, and Tanya said, 'There's mine, too.' I looked at our group now hammer-ing in a windbreak and saw that along with Tim, Archie and Harry there was a fourth boy – Ivan, Tanya's boring brother.

'Do you want to come?' I said to Cat.

'No, I'm fine,' she said. 'I'll wait for Matt and the others. He can buy me some lunch. He's loaded.' (I refrained from pointing out that he didn't have enough money to buy his own cigarettes.)

'I think it's disgusting. It looks like a large, pus-filled whitehead,' Ivan was waxing lyrical about Cat's nose stud.

'And you would know, of course,' said Tanya scathingly to her older brother. 'Personally I think it's wicked.'

'I think it looks quite pretty.' Dear old lovesick Harry. If only he knew how far removed from his orbit Cat was these days.

'I read a magazine article all about piercing,' said Archie. 'People do it for the most bizarre reasons—'

My brother joined in. 'And people get the most bizarre parts of their bodies pierced—'

'That's enough, Tim,' said my mother. 'Have a chipolata and be quiet.' Needless to say, all six of us teenagers fell about laughing. I wished Cat was with us, though. I sort of missed her. In the old days she would have joined in our picnic and regaled us all with her fantastic tales that no one ever quite believed – except for Harry of course. Cat's parents aren't really beach people. They've always been happy for her to spend the day with us while they explored the local towns and gardens, or went on cliff walks. I sat with my sandwich and a packet of crisps and observed the others. I almost wished I had my sketchbook with me, except that I don't like people looking at it. Tanya sat leaning against a rock. She's on the solid side, with fairish hair, liquid brown eyes and, despite her gloomy nature, a mouth that curls readily into a smile. Ivan's hair is cut very short, but he's got the same eyes, magnified behind glasses, and the curly-lipped smile too. And of course he sports the famous earring. Sadly it would take more than an earring to make Ivan look cool.

Harry and Archie are sailing types like their father. You see them everywhere from Norfolk to Cornwall, and they come in all ages and sizes. Dark wavy hair, blue eyes and usually navy-blue jerseys and jeans. The boys will be nice-looking when they're older but at the moment they're both *so* painfully straight. Now an earring could make a difference to the way Harry looks. Perhaps I should suggest it. It might make Cat look on him more kindly.

'How's the music going, Ivan?' asked my dad as he came round offering more sandwiches.

'Oh don't get him started,' said Tanya.

'Good, thanks,' said Ivan. 'They're starting the scratch choir on Friday for a concert on Sunday. Anyone interested?'

'Don't be daft!' said Tanya. 'Who wants to sing hymns in a cold old church when they could be on the beach?'

'My sentiments precisely,' I said with a warning glance at Dad. He knows I don't like to talk about music in front of my friends.

'Well, all I can say is, plenty of people,' said Dad. 'And it's not hymns, Tanya, it's choral works, Handel and so on.'

'Same difference,' said Tanya contemptuously. She looked wistfully over to where Cat was sitting with Matt and the other three. 'Bet they're not discussing classical music,' she said.

I peered in their direction. I could just make out Cat and Matt snuggled up together on a towel. Liza and Sebastian were still at the chasing each other around stage. Paul and Luke arrived from somewhere with some cans. They sat down and handed them round. Matt sat up and I could see him offering round a pack of cigarettes.

'Did you hire a board this morning?' Dad asked.

'Yes,' I said quickly.

'No you didn't,' said Tanya. 'I never saw you go off and hire a board.'

'You weren't there all the time, Tanya. It was when you'd gone off with Liza somewhere.'

'Oh yeah. We went to the loo didn't we?' (When I bought the cigarettes.) 'And the surf shop to look at swimsuits.' (When I'd borrowed Cat's board). 'I'd forgotten that.' (Phew.)

'And I expect you spent the rest on drinks and ice-creams, didn't you?' said Dad, indulgent as ever.

'You spoil our daughter,' said Mum. 'Don't forget you still owe me for that bracelet.'

'I won't forget, Mum.' Cat didn't have to put up with this sort of stuff. 'Shall we go back and join the others, Tanya?'

'I'll come too,' said Ivan.

'No you won't,' said Tanya.

We spent the rest of the afternoon lazing around on the beach. I was still borrowing Cat's board, so we alternated our turns in the sea and I didn't see much of her or Matt. 'Are you going back home before going out again?' I asked her.

'Yeah,' she said. 'Expect one of my parents to ask yours if you can be at the pub with me. I expect we'll get a lift. You know the score, don't you?'

'It's cool,' I said, smiling at Matt in an understanding way.

'That's the point, Dad. Everyone's there. We can all keep an eye on each other. We're only sitting outside drinking Coke.' (A small lie to spare the olds.) 'The good thing about Cat's parents being worried is that they'll come and get us. Except they won't try and drive past – we'll meet them in the top car park at eleven.'

'I want you home by eleven-fifteen.'

'Yes, Dad.'

'And that doesn't mean you can come in that late every night.'

'Da-ad!'

I ran out to where Cat was leaning on the horn. It was just her and me for now. There was a slim chance that Tanya and Liza would come later with Ellie and friends.

'One thing, Cat,' I said, as we scanned the crowds for Matt.

'Mmm?'

'You have to pay for my drink. I haven't got any money left."

'Oh OK,' she said, in that offhand way she has sometimes. 'Matt will pay, I'm sure.'

The crowd parted. Matt, Luke, Sebastian and Paul had arrived. This was just so cool. 'Hi guys,' I said with my new smile that showed off my lips but not my teeth.

'Matt, give me some money,' said Cat. 'I'm going to buy the drinks.'

'Just don't get caught,' said Matt.

'You and Josie bag that bit of wall,' said Cat. 'I won't be a sec.'

I was left sitting on the wall with Matt. The other three were standing up, talking amongst themselves. It was chillier than before. I pulled my jacket round me. Matt offered me one of my cigarettes. I took one and let him light it for me. I tried to smoke it without coughing.

'I know you want to be with Cat tonight,' I said. 'I don't mind covering for her.' Ms Nice Guy, me. Matt didn't respond. 'Sometimes,' I said, 'two people just have to be alone together. I appreciate that. I mean, I just love being on my own with a guy. The freedom to do what you want. Be uninhibited.'

'You're a nice kid, you know?' said Matt, but he wasn't able to say any more because Cat arrived with the drinks. Mine was a Coke. I was going to have to make it last quite a long time, three hours to be precise. Cat and Matt knocked back theirs and disappeared. I was left sitting in the middle of a circle of standing guys.

'Why don't you sit down?' I said.

'Oh, OK,' said Paul, and sat. 'Go and get some more drinks, Luke. What do you want Josie? Still on the Archers like last time?' He didn't give me a chance to say no. I was enjoying myself. It was great being with this popular group. Other girls cast envious glances, I could tell. At last. Despite my brace, I was surrounded by three amazingly cool surfers. I wished my friends from home could see me. And for once I wasn't stuck with Ivan and Harry, or Seth. Luke brought me two Archers, to save time! How thoughtful! And then they all talked to me – about Cat, about me, about themselves. They asked me all about the boyfriends I'd had in the past. I had to improvise a bit. I pretended something had really happened with the drummer on the music course, and I invented a longterm boyfriend (I called him Tim, after my brother – the first name that came to mind!).

'Quite a girl, eh?' said Luke to Sebastian, when I'd finished.

'Of course, Tim was very passionate about me,' I said. 'He was devastated when we finished. We'd had such an – intense – relationship, for as long as I can remember.' (That was true. I have had an intense relationship with my wretched little brother as long as I can remember.) Two more Archers later, and a lot of cigarettes, I can't remember what I was telling them.

At ten to eleven Cat and Matt came back. I was very relieved to see her. I'd been worried about what to do if she didn't turn up. She had bright red spots on her cheeks and she looked quite upset. 'You OK, Cat?'

'Why shouldn't I be?' she said sharply. 'Just going to the loo, Josie, and then we'll go and meet the beloved parent.'

My head was spinning a bit. I tried to organise my brain, ready for Cat's dad. I heard the boys talking, but I didn't really grasp the implications of what they were saying.

'Well?' Sebastian was asking Matt.

In reply, Matt just gave a thumbs down sign. He looked rather sad. I felt quite sorry for him. Cat came back, more her old self.

'Bye, gorgeous,' she said over her shoulder to Matt, and linked her arm in mine. She hauled me up the hill to the car park where the car was already waiting for us. I found it a great effort putting one foot in front of the other. 'Now remember,' she hissed, 'I was there all the flaming time.' I rehearsed my line as we climbed.

'Cat was there *all* the flaming time,' I said slowly and carefully to her dad, and promptly threw up in the hedge.

Five

I was in trouble, big trouble. Not with Cat – I'd covered for her, and even taken the heat off her for the time being. But my parents – wo-oh!

Next morning: 'Josephine, you have completely abused our trust in you. I am very disappointed,' said my dad.

'Drinking *and* smoking!' said my mum.

'You are aware,' said Dad severely, 'that under-age drinking is illegal? That you could be putting the landlord's licence at risk? His livelihood?'

'And how come you were so ill and Cat wasn't?' asked Mum. 'Good friends look after each other. I don't think these boys are very good friends either.'

Actually it was Tim who came to my rescue – a bit. 'Lighten up, you two,' he said. 'Don't you think you're overreacting? She only went to the pub, for God's sake! Everyone else does. At least she's not getting stoned out of her brain down at the campsite.'

'Well, she's not going again, is all I can say,' said Dad, and went off, grumbling, to make some coffee.

'I'm sorry,' I said feebly. 'The boys bought me drinks and they just kept on coming. I started off with a Coke, honest.'

Mum relaxed a bit with Dad out of the room. 'Let's hope you've learned your lesson, darling. At least you've come out of it safely. You'll probably never want that particular drink again. But don't smoke, sweetheart. It'll ruin your voice.'

'It was only one or two, Mum. I can't believe you didn't try things out when you were my age.'

'That doesn't mean I can stand by and watch when you're being silly.'

'All right, Mum. I really am sorry. Have we got anything for headaches?'

'Go back to bed. I'll bring you something. But it will take a while for your father to calm down. It's probably better if you're out of the way.'

I cuddled Monk for comfort and slept half the morning, so I felt normal by the time I was properly awake. I sat up and reached for my sketchbook. I drew the view through my low window. A thrush had been sitting amongst the roses that stretched across the sill, so I drew that too. I fingered my dolphin bracelet and stayed in bed, enjoying the solitude. I felt a list coming on, a private, personal list:

Reasons why Matt might be attracted to me
My hair
My figure (I'm slim, look OK in a bikini)
I'm generous
I'm sympathetic
I'm experienced (he thinks)
I'm popular (ie Cat likes me)

Reasons why Matt might not be attracted to me
BRACE
Young
No good at surfing
(No good at anything much!)
Actually, not that popular

As you might conclude, I fancy Matt. I admit it. I know he's Cat's boyfriend and everything, but he's dead nice to me, and he didn't look that happy about her last night. Perhaps she'd dumped him or something. She said goodnight to him, but she didn't kiss him or anything. I'd have to ask her what was going on, very tactfully of course. I shut the sketchbook. Then I panicked in case anyone picked it up and frantically scribbled out the name Matt and put a question mark there instead, so it read *Reasons?* ~~Matt~~ *might be attracted to me.* After all, Cat is quite capable of walking in here any time. I pushed Monk under the duvet for the same reason.

I couldn't remember that much about last night after about the second drink. I know the boys were interested in me, trying to find out about me. I'm not used to being the centre of attention! I remember vaguely looking out for the dolphin boys. They were there some of the time.

I was aware of the respectful way people seemed to treat them, as they stood outside the door gazing out to sea. Very romantic!

Cat was running up the stairs, calling 'Josie! Time to move your ass!' I shoved the sketchbook (lucky I'd scratched out Matt's name!) down the bed with Monk, and slid back under the duvet.

'I'm surprised they let you in,' I said.

'What do you mean?'

'Might you just be considered something of a bad influence round here?'

'Nah. Not any more. I saw your dad, said I was sorry I hadn't looked after you better. You hadn't really had much to drink, perhaps you had a stomach bug or something.'

'And he bought it?'

'He didn't stop me coming in.'

'Good. That means he's calmed down. I'm not allowed to go tonight though.'

'I'll have to ask Liza or Tanya then.' (Gee, thanks, Cat.) 'But we're planning a beach party tomorrow night! You'll have to come to that. Surely your mum and dad wouldn't say no?'

'I'll have to work on them. I'm on best behaviour now.'

'Get up then. Come down to the beach.'

'The surfing beach?'

'No. This one. We can sunbathe.'

'Is Matt going to be there?'

'Oh yes. We'll all be there.' She got up from my bed. 'You can ride pillion on my bike if no one gives us a lift. Come and get me when you're ready.'

As soon as I went downstairs I gave my dad a hug. I don't like upsetting him. 'Sorry, Daddy.' He said something gruff and unintelligible but I knew I was basically forgiven. 'Where is everyone?'

'They've taken the little ones to the bay.'

Easy does it. 'Can I go to the beach with Cat?'

'I suppose she can't lead you into any trouble down there. Mum left us some sandwiches, so make yourself a picnic. And I want you back by six. Mum's got the mobile, so just make sure you're not late, or I'll have to think seriously about letting you do things with your friends.'

'Thanks, Dad.' I think he must have assumed Cat's parents would drive us – he really doesn't realise how independent she is. I gathered up my stuff and went over to Cat's. We went round the side way so Dad wouldn't see me riding pillion on Cat's bike. We caught up with Seth on his skateboard half way down. I reminded myself that Cat thought he was a bit weird and prepared myself not to take any notice of him, but Cat seemed to have forgotten herself.

'So-o-o dangerous!' squealed Cat as we overtook him.

'I kno-o-ow!' he shrieked back, laughing.

We found everyone else in the dunes. There was a huge bunch of kids, including Liza and Tanya and even Ivan.

'Hi guys!' said Cat. 'It's me!' (You have to be very self-assured to say that sort of thing.)

'We all heard what you got up to last night!' said Ivan. Cat gave me an anxious glance before she realised it was my notoriety up for discussion, not hers. She went over to Matt. The others all said hi, but he barely acknowledged her. What had she done to upset him?

Seth turned up and sat beside me. I tried to act aloof. 'Heard about last night!' he said. Cat glanced over and looked relieved when she realised Seth was also referring to me and not her. It made me wonder again – what had she been up to? I felt slightly wistful for other summers when we'd told each other everything, even if it had only been about Seth and Harry and Ivan (well, not really Ivan), and the bike hire boy.

'What I want to know, Seth, is *how* everyone heard about last night,' I said. 'Cat?' I called over to her. 'What have you been saying about me?'

'I certainly didn't say anything to Seth or Ivan,' she said, as if she wouldn't have bothered speaking to them.

I suppose I didn't altogether want Matt to think I was comfortable consorting with a ten-foot ginger rastafarian either, so I got up and went to join Cat and the lads. I mean, Seth's OK in private, but it was different being seen with him in public. 'So who did you tell?' I asked, trying to make a joke of it.

'I might have mentioned it to Tanya,' she said. 'She and Liza couldn't make it last night, so they wanted to know.' Liza was schmoozing with Sebastian, I noticed. Tanya was looking resigned with Paul. That left Luke. I was glad I'd moved over here. Seth and Ivan were really pretty sad. They looked like weirdos.

Luke was quite friendly. People came and went, but our little group stayed put. It was neat, really. Cat and Matt, Liza and Sebastian, Tanya and Paul, me and Luke (except that I fancied Matt and Tanya didn't think much of Paul).

'So, Josie,' said Luke, 'how do you know Cat?'

'Her cottage is just behind ours,' I said.

'You're quite a pair, I gather. You and Cat.'

'Oh yes,' I said, though I didn't quite know what he was talking about. 'Anyway. How about you? How do you four know each other?'

'From school,' he said. 'We've been planning this holiday for ages. My parents are staying further down the coast, but we persuaded them to let us camp and surf here.' That was the first time any of them had mentioned parents. They seemed so grown-up. 'Matt said it would be a brilliant way to – er – meet girls. He was right!'

'Have you all got girlfriends at home?'

'Only Matt—' he said, and then stopped. 'Of course we have. Though not right now.' He laughed nervously when I looked at him. Actually, he had a nice smile. When I first met the boys it was, like, Matt – the best-looking by far – and three others, with Paul and his big ears definitely the least attractive. Matt has classic gorgeous features, short dark hair, chiselled cheekbones, green eyes. Sebastian and Luke just look like hunky surfers, with longish, light-coloured hair. Sebastian is the fairer of the two, with blond eyebrows and stubble. Luke looks slightly younger with a more girlish skin – and the nice smile. That's why it was Sebastian who got to buy the drinks. Actually Paul's not that bad. It's just that he has these rather thin features and short hair, which make his ears look worse. He and Tanya seemed to be getting on fine now. He was writing something on her plaster cast. Something witty – it made her laugh.

I didn't want Matt to think I was being too friendly

with Luke. Cat was lying on her front and he was leaning back against a dune, one hand stroking her back (I noticed with envy) and the other holding a cigarette. But they weren't talking to each other. In fact, I reckoned he was watching me quite a lot.

'Anyone coming for a swim?' I said brightly. There was no reply. Cat seemed to be asleep and Tanya and Liza were annointing one another with sun tan lotion.

'OK, we'll come, won't we?' said Matt to the other boys, and they went ahead of me down into the water. I swam around to keep warm but they floated about chatting to each other. I couldn't help earwigging their conversation.

'How are you getting on with yours?' Sebastian asked Paul.

'Better, now you've let me switch!' said Paul. 'And I don't have to ask you – it's obvious!'

'That's because you let me switch, too!' said Sebastian.

'Matt messed up, didn't he? He thought he would be miles in the lead by now.'

'Don't let him hear you say that!'

I quickly swam in the opposite direction. What were they on about? Amazing how they respected Matt – 'don't let him hear you say that'. I was nearest to him now. I nearly drowned just gazing at his muscles. Wow. I'd give anything to swap places with Cat.

Then Matt said something that really surprised me. 'Let's go surfing. I'm not going to get those points with her, am I?' Was he talking about Cat? I was forced to duck and swim underwater to get further away so they wouldn't think I was listening. I popped up where I couldn't hear them at all. Actually I'd heard enough (though I wasn't sure I liked what I'd heard), and I'd swum enough too – I was quite cold. So I went back to our place in the dunes alone, wondering if the four boys would stay after their swim or do something different.

Tanya, Liza and Cat were all lying on their fronts either sleeping or reading. Seth and Ivan were playing a game of football with a beer can. Ivan said hi, but Seth seemed intent on ignoring me, which hurt. I flopped down by Cat. Had Matt been talking about her? I had to get to the bottom of it. I nudged her. 'Cat? You look as though you're burning. I'll put lotion on your back if you'll do mine.' I started on her back anyway – it was looking rather pink. 'Is – everything OK with Matt?'

'Yes,' she said lightly, too lightly.

'Cat? What's the matter?'

'Nothing. It's fine really. We're cool.' She rubbed lotion into my back vigorously.

The boys came back and said they were going back to the campsite and then surfing. Cat said she'd follow them on her bike. Seth said he'd join them too and I was left with Tanya, Ivan and Liza and a long walk back to Tredunnet. In fact it was a long walk back with Liza because Tanya and Ivan were meeting up with their parents and going somewhere else.

Liza was bubbling over. 'This holiday is turning out so brilliant!' she said, 'and I really thought I was going to be forced to spend it with my sister and her friends. There's nothing wrong with them – they're just older, but none of them are half as cool as Sebastian! I think I'm in love!'

'We're so lucky, aren't we?' I said. 'And Tanya seems quite keen on Paul, too.'

'He's nice, despite the way he looks. And Tanya's hardly the most beautiful girl in the world, is she?'

'Liza!'

'Well, it's true. She'd be the first to acknowledge it. What's Luke like?'

I didn't want to talk about Luke. He was nice but I didn't have any feelings for him – not like I did about Matt. Just then two boys came down the hill on bicycles. It was the dolphin boys! There was something so special about them. 'Who are those boys, Liza? Do you know anything about them?'

'No, but everyone else seems to. Everyone goes up and talks to them at the pub. I've seen them surfing too. I'll try and find out. Sebastian's bound to know.'

'Matt will, I expect.' There, I'd said his name. 'Liza – is everything all right with Cat and Matt?'

Liza giggled. 'Everything except their names! Cat sat on the Matt!'

'Has she said anything about last night? I know I was out of it, but she didn't look at all happy when she came back to the pub.'

'What do you mean?'

Oops. Blown it. But it would be nice to share this particular problem. 'Last night. I was covering for her while she went off to Matt's tent with him. Then she could tell her dad she'd been with me at the pub all along.'

Liza stopped in her tracks. 'Blimey. I didn't realise that's what she was up to. I *suppose* she knows what she's doing. I'm not sure that I would have wanted to be her alibi.'

'I'm her best friend. I had to.'

'Hmmm.'

'She wouldn't tell me what they did.'

'Honestly Josie, would you expect her to? I assume it was either sex or drugs, or both.'

'Do you think so? I just thought she and Matt wanted some time alone together. It didn't seem too much to ask.'

'Well, let's hope you're right.'

'What would you do if Sebastian asked you back to his tent?'

'I'd think hard about it first. I might be a bit scared actually.'

'You know Cat. She doesn't scare easily. Think how brave she must have been to have the nose stud. I screamed when I had my ears pierced. Mind you, nothing could be as bad as these train tracks.'

'I kind of wish you hadn't told me about Cat. I said I'd keep her company at the pub tonight, but then I'm dying to be with Sebastian again. You should get together with Luke. He's nice. Four of us and four of them – sorted! How about the beach barbecue tomorrow? Go on, go for it! You know you want to!'

We'd reached the point where we went our separate ways. I felt funny after my conversation with Liza. Had I been wrong to cover for Cat? And why did I have to fancy Matt when it would have been so much better all round to go for Luke?

That evening I felt bad about Seth too. I heard him scooting uphill on his skateboard at one point and thought how nice it might have been to go round to his cottage tonight and carry on with his songs. In fact I was experiencing something of a remorse-fest. I didn't like myself very much. How could I even be slightly interested in my best friend's boyfriend? But then I'd heard him say weird things about her. What sort of 'points' were they talking about? I went up to my room after supper and drew pictures of dolphins, which calmed me down a bit. I'd so love to talk to the dolphin boys – pity they're way out of my league.

My parents were off to a concert with my uncle and aunt and David. Harry and Archie came over to help us babysit my little cousins. Tim produced a pack of cards and a box of Smarties. 'We play for Smarties, OK?' and a daft game got under way. Archie got hiccups and had to be bashed very thoroughly. We made so much noise that my cousins came downstairs to join in. We ended up playing charades. 'Jaw-ass-sick-Park' was my cousins' favourite, though they just romped around pretending to be dinosaurs. Tim made me act 'sick'. Harry got it straight away. News travels fast.

'Tell me again why you and Cat were both sick in the pub last night?' said Harry. Anything to talk about Cat.

'Only *I* was sick! And we'd left the pub. Cat wasn't even there. She wasn't at the pub!' Oops. Done it again.

'So where was Cat? I heard her parents telling Dad she was fine because she was with you.'

'Ah. Well. Yes, she was sort of with me.'

'Get your story straight, Josie,' said my brother. 'People keep asking me, too.'

'OK. Promise you won't tell anyone? I was Cat's alibi, so I stayed at the pub while she went off with Matt, her boyfriend.'

'Don't say any more,' said Harry. 'I don't want to

55

know. I've never spoken to this Matt person and I'm not sure that I want to. I suppose he's really cool.'

'He's got an earring,' I said, thinking it was never too early to plant the seeds.

'So's Ivan,' said Archie. 'But that doesn't make him cool.'

'Nothing would make Ivan cool,' said Tim. 'You'd look good with an earring Harry. Maybe you and I should go together. There's a place in Newquay. Gideon was telling me.'

'Who's Gideon?' the rest of us asked together.

'Gideon and Caleb – surely you've seen them?'

We all looked blank.

'They're brothers. They go around together. Fair hair.'

The dolphin boys! Gideon and Caleb. Such romantic names. But already my heart was set only on Matt.

Later I drew a three-quarter portrait from memory of Matt's head and shoulders, with slick wet hair and goose-bumps on the skin of his biceps. I was so jealous of Cat. I tried not to think about the two of them together.

Six

At breakfast Tim was full of it. He'd already heard it from Seth who'd heard it from Ivan who'd got it first-hand from Tanya. I don't know, these sad boys who get up early and gossip! Cat had been caught out. I couldn't wait to go over and hear all the details.

Dad was full of something, too. The concert in the little church had been wonderful. And there was the art exhibition next door. They always set aside an area for 'children's work'. Dad thought I ought to do something for it.

'Probably not, Dad. I don't really wait to sit and paint on this holiday.'

'Think how proud you'd be to have your work displayed for all to see during the interval of the concert.'

'I'm not going to be in the concert either this year.'

'Oh Jo-jo. I was hoping we could still persuade you to sing.'

'No. No way.'

I ran over to Cat's. She was just getting into their car. 'See you at the barbecue, Josie!' she said cheerfully. 'Half-past seven! Bring a potato or something!' Her dad shut her door for her and directed a grim nod of greeting at me before driving off. I went on to Tanya's, half hoping I could meet Seth and make up with him on the way. But there was no sign of him.

Tanya's parents were delivering Ivan to the church, and picking up some shopping, so she was on her own. She was perched on a stool in her dressing-gown, eating toast and vaguely watching breakfast television. 'Hey, Josie! You missed a whole lot of drama last night.'

'And you're dying to tell me about it.' I pulled up another stool and waited expectantly.

'OK. Well, we were down at the pub last night, sitting on the wall outside like good little girls and boys. Liza and I had our nice soft drinks.' (I felt envious already.

That was all I had wanted the other night. Just fun and good company.) 'I'm really beginning to like Paul, and Liza and Sebastian are pretty much an item. Luke was a bit lonely! But Cat and Matt were going to do their disappearing trick. Liza actually tried to talk her out of it, but Cat said she knew what she was doing. Matt seemed pretty grumpy to me, actually, but he cheered up a bit and waved to all his friends as Cat dragged him off.'

Tanya clomped over in her cast to pour some tea and carried on. 'So it was all hunky-dory. My brother and Seth even stopped off for a bit. Luke told them about the barbecue tomorrow, which hacked me off – I *so* don't want my brother there, but what can you do? They were chatting with some other lads and then disappeared. But THEN, at about ten o'clock—' Tanya got up and poured yet another cup of tea. She was really laying on the suspense – 'Cat's dad appeared. He marched past us and went into the pub. When he came out again, he said, "Has anyone seen Catherine? She led me to believe she would be here." Panic stations. We all faffed about, didn't know what to say. Then Luke said, sweet as pie, "I think Matthew had left his wallet behind and they popped back to fetch it. They'll be here in a minute I'm sure." "Popped where?" says Cat's dad. He's ever so suspicious. "To the campsite," says Sebastian, who hasn't quite sized up the situation. "Well, she'd better be on her way back," says her dad, "because I'm driving over to meet her right now!" Exit Cat's dad.'

'So what did you all do?'

'Quick as a flash, Luke used his mobile to ring Matt on his. Luckily, Matt picked up, Luke just told them to get straight back here – the story was that Matt had left his wallet behind.'

'So did Cat get away with it?'

'We didn't see her, because her dad drove her straight home. Matt said it had been a close thing, though he wouldn't exactly tell us why. The guys all sniggered a lot. But he said Cat play-acted like mad with her dad – "Oh Daddy, we'd only just nipped out to get Matt's wallet, etcetera, etcetera." My lift appeared soon after, so that's all I know. Liza stayed on awhile – she might know more. Let's go over to her house. I'll just put some clothes on. I had a wash earlier – can't even have a shower with this flaming thing on my leg.'

We went down the road to Liza's. It's quite a shock when you go in the door of an ordinary-sized holiday house to see all these millions of boys milling round in their boxer shorts. I felt quite embarrassed, but none of them seemed to mind.

'We want you to tell us what happened after I left the pub last night,' said Tanya, leading Liza out onto a patio at the side that was off the boys' beaten track between tents and kitchen.

Liza had a dreamy expression on her face. 'Sebastian kissed me,' she said. She was obviously still on Cloud Nine. 'He said he was crazy about me. He even likes my hair!' She ran her hands through her thick, tangled mop. (He must be keen.) 'I can't wait for the barbecue this evening. We can't see each other before then because of some surfing competition they're all doing first.'

'Seth's doing that too,' said Tanya. 'But tell us about Matt. What did he say about Cat's dad and everything?'

'He said Cat's dad wasn't too pleased. More or less

accused him of leading Cat on, pushing drugs, blah blah.'

I pictured Matt's beautiful troubled face as he was so unjustly picked on and my heart bled for him. But then I suddenly felt naive. 'Is that what they were doing? Smoking dope?'

'Quite likely,' said Liza matter-of-factly. 'People do, you know.'

'Do *you*?' I asked, wide-eyed. My cosy world was cracking slightly.

'No, as it happens, but I can't vouch for anyone else in this madhouse.' Liza always seems so sorted. It must come from having an older sister and understanding parents.

'Anyway, Cat's coming to the barbecue tonight,' I said. 'I saw her going off this morning and she told me.'

'OK guys. So how shall we pass the time until then?' said Tanya.

'Not so fast, Tanya,' said Liza. 'I want to hear more about you and Paul. How's it going?'

'So-so. He wouldn't have much luck dragging me and my peg leg off to his tent for an evening of passion – it would take us all evening to get there!'

'I wouldn't go anyway,' said Liza. 'I bet their tent's disgusting. You should see inside some of the ones in our garden! Their sleeping bags stink. They wear the same underpants for days before leaving them lying around. Plus damp socks. Beer cans. Cigarette stubs. Nasty.'

I kept quiet. There's obviously so much I don't know. Secretly I felt pretty sure I'd go anywhere with Matt if it made him happy.

'Now I've given you the lowdown on Paul,' said Tanya. 'What's it to be for us? Girly morning?'

It's funny – although I've always known these two, this is the first summer I've felt part of the crowd. It's been me and Cat some of the time, and me and my old playmates – Harry, Archie and Seth – the rest. But the whole thing of the four of us girls is just so brilliant, and it's all because of Matt and his friends. They've made the holiday so much more fun. I thought for a moment about the 'holiday romance' that I'd promised to have. That was a tricky one. As far as I was concerned, there was only one candidate, and he was taken.

'We could go shopping,' Liza suggested.

'I need to buy some postcards and presents for my friends,' said Tanya. 'Let's do that.'

'How are we going to get you there?' asked Liza.

'Wait for my parents to get back and then make them drive us to the ferry. I can walk around the shops if you lot don't mind going slowly.'

'I'll have to ask my parents first,' I said. 'Don't go without me will you?'

'See you back at my house,' said Tanya. 'Don't be too long.'

Once in a while I wish someone here would say: 'Please come with us, Josie. It won't be any fun without you. We'll wait for you – for as long as it takes.' That sort of thing. Holly, my friend at home, would. Perhaps it's my brace. Perhaps it makes me look young and they don't want to be seen with me. That's the downside of being in with a popular group. You're always having to keep up. It feels like hard work sometimes. And now three of us have got boyfriends. And the fourth – me – hasn't.

'Good idea, darling,' said my mother. 'Good opportunity to spend some of your holiday money. By the way, you still owe me £1.50. How about giving it to me now, so we're square?'

I could just about scrape that amount together, with the change from the fiver and some silver I found in a pocket, but it left me completely and utterly stony broke again. I gave Mum the money. It was worth it to stop her going on about it. 'Would you pay for my ferry fare?' I asked tentatively.

'I suppose that comes under expenses,' she said. 'Here it is exactly. Remember to hang on to the return fare too.' Huh. I'd have to, because I didn't have any other money.

'Did Dad tell you about the art exhibition?' Mum asked. 'Do one of your clever paintings and you might even make some money!'

I hadn't thought of that aspect. 'I'll think about it. Mum, I have to go – I'm worried the others won't wait. But please, *pleasepleaseplease*, can I go to a barbecue down on the beach tonight? Everyone's going.'

'I expect so,' she said. 'We'll ask Dad when you get back. Convince him that you'll stay out of the way of temptation. I think he reckons it's time to give you another chance.'

I raced over to Tanya's. I needn't have hurried. Her dad was having a cup of coffee before he turned round and went out again. Tanya and Liza were comparing how much money they had to spend. Before they could ask me, I said I was only going to buy something if I really really wanted it. I was mulling over the idea of doing a painting and selling it. If I could sell it over the weekend it would solve my money problems for the rest of the holiday.

The ferry is a lovely little boat that leaves from the beach here and drops you in the middle of girly shoppers' paradise on the other side. We cruised round jewellery shops, shell shops, card shops, gift shops. The other two bought loads. I tried to focus on what I might be able to buy next week. I even saw the perfect present for Holly, but I would just have to be patient. It was hot, and what I wanted most was an ice-cream. I didn't want to tell them I'd come shopping with no money, so I just had to grin and bear it when they assumed I didn't want one, and bought gorgeous, mouthwatering ice-creams for themselves.

We were on the return ferry when Liza started nudging and giggling. 'Hey,' she whispered. 'Don't look round straight away, but at some point turn your heads and cop a load of two really fit guys. They even put my lovely Sebastian in the shade.'

'Wouldn't take much to put Paul in the shade,' said Tanya, but we both turned our heads simultaneously and saw – the dolphin boys. 'I've seen them at the pub,' she said. 'I think Paul knows them. They're surfers. Dead cool. What do you think, Josie?'

I wanted to show off my inside knowledge and say that I knew their names, but I couldn't because I'd caught the younger one's sea-grey gaze and it had rendered me speechless. We'd anyway arrived on the home side and the skipper was helping us off the boat and Tanya was phoning for a lift.

*

'Did you buy anything?' called my mum as I went upstairs.

'Not today,' I called back. I'd had the idea that Dad might be more inclined to let me go to the barbecue if I was more amenable about the painting. I turned to a fresh page of my sketchbook and stared at it. Then I looked at my drawing of a boy morphing into a dolphin. Maybe I could do something with that if I used colour. Sea colours. All sea colours. I sat and sketched for half an hour. Suddenly I was ravenous. The others had bought pasties, but I'd had to decline again. I went downstairs and started making a sandwich.

'Didn't you have any lunch?' asked Mum. A bit of quick thinking. 'Yes, I had a pasty. Had to pay for it myself.'

'I'll pay you back for that. I should've thought.' So now I had £1.75. And I'd paid Mum back for the bracelet. Things were looking up.

'Did you say anything to Dad about me going to the barbecue?'

'I haven't had a chance – he's been out with your uncle's lot and Tim all morning. He's getting over your antics the other night but he's still quite upset about you not doing a picture *or* singing in the concert.'

'I've changed my mind about the picture. In fact, I've already started sketching.'

'But that's marvellous. Dad will be thrilled. He's so proud of you, you know!'

'No need to go over the top, Mum. Just say I can go to the barbecue.'

'I'll certainly make a very strong case for you.'

'Thanks. You've got four hours.' Which meant I had four hours too. To decide what to wear, shower, change, make up, etc. I nipped over to Cat's but she wasn't back yet. Tanya was round at Liza's. I called in there. The two of them were still at the deciding-what-to-wear-stage, so I joined in. 'Anyone can borrow my stuff if they want,' I offered.

'Your clothes wouldn't fit me,' said Tanya, blunt as always.

'I don't even know what *sort* of clothes to wear,' said Liza. It was a beautiful clear, sunny afternoon. It looked set fair for a beautiful summer evening too.

'Trousers, nice top, plus blouse or something,' I said. 'We are on the beach, after all.'

'I'd thought maybe bikini and sarong,' said Liza.

'Midges,' I said. 'Better to be covered up a bit.'

'I agree,' said Tanya. 'Though I don't think Paul would give a stuff what I wore.'

'Ooo-ooh, I wish I knew what Sebastian expected!'

'As few clothes as possible I imagine,' said Tanya, 'but you don't have to dress to please him. Be comfortable, that's far more important!'

'Exactly,' I said. But I was worried now. I knew I'd dress to please Matt if I only knew how, Cat or no Cat. Perhaps 'as little as possible' was the answer.

'I wish Cat was back,' said Liza. 'She's brilliant on make-up. And she'd know exactly what to wear. I've got this cool dress I'd put on if I knew other people were dressing up.'

'Short or long?' said Tanya.

'Short. Show off a bit of thigh.'

I had a short skirt, kind of silvery, and a bit

inappropriate for the beach – but if Liza was wearing a short dress . . .

'I think you should go for the nearly-naked look, Liza,' said Tanya. 'That's what men like, isn't it? I wish Cat was back too. She's got the most experience with boys. I'd ask Ivan straight out, but we all know his opinion would be worse than useless. It's bad enough that he's coming.'

'What about Seth?' I asked. 'He might know.'

'You must be joking,' said Tanya. 'He's almost as bad as Ivan.'

'Oh, I don't know,' said Liza. 'Seth has a certain style, in a new age, surfie kind of way. He's been here for months. He might have been to other beach barbies.'

'I'll go and ask him,' I volunteered. I was anxious to be friends with Seth before tonight. And I needed to go back home and reassess my wardrobe for the naked look. 'I'll call in on Cat, too. How are you two getting down to the beach?'

'Lift, I expect,' said Tanya. 'Sometimes it's good to have your leg in plaster!'

'I'll go down with Cat,' I said. 'If she's in, we'll come over.'

Cat wasn't in. That was strange. I thought she'd have *forced* her parents, at gunpoint if necessary, to get her back in time to change for the barbecue. I slogged on up the hill to Seth's, praying he'd be up from the beach. I stood in the porch and knocked on the kitchen door of the crowded little cottage. Wind-chimes jingled in the breeze off the sea. I peered in to a tumbling litter of small children. Then I saw Seth stepping over them. He opened the door, and looked down on me from his great gangly height. 'So what brings you here?' he asked, guardedly.

'Seth, I'm sorry I was a bit offhand yesterday. Don't know what came over me.'

'The presence of better-looking guys, I suspect,' said Seth.

'I shouldn't have been like that. It's just that I – I really like one of them.'

'Oh yeah?' said Seth. 'I won't ask which one. I dare say all will be revealed down on the beach tonight.' He coughed. 'Anyway, gotta go, man. I'm helping to build the bonfire, gather driftwood and stuff.'

'You've done this before?'

'Yeah, man. Lots of times.'

'I know it's a silly question, Seth, but what did people wear?'

Seth hooted with laughter. 'Not a lot!' he said. He ducked back into the cottage for his guitar and slung it on his back. Then he came into the porch again and picked up his skateboard. 'Check out my beach gear,' he said holding out his arms, 'style guru that I am! Don't ask me about clothes, Jo-jo. I don't even care about the right labels. Ask one of your cool guys. Bye! See you later!' I watched him glide down the hill, still not quite sure if we were friends.

I tried Cat again before going home. Still no one there. Home. My lot were all back. 'So what's this about a party on the beach tonight?' said Dad.

'Just a barbecue, Dad. Everyone else is going. Good clean fun, don't you know?'

'I know. Mum told me. Well, it just means all the

more supper for us up here! You can go, Jo-jo, but I don't want you staying out until all hours.'

'What's your problem, Dad? Surely you can't object to a barbecue on the beach with all my friends? Or aren't I supposed to have any fun on holiday? It's practically Sunday-school-outing stuff.' I was beginning to get exercised, but luckily Dad was in a benign mood.

'It's OK, darling. Alan and Pat are going to the pub down there later on. Alan's said he'll run you home – and any of your friends who need a lift.' I thought better of objecting, and went upstairs to rethink my clothes for the evening.

On the bed I'd laid out my Jeffrey Rogers trousers and the new top from the surf shop, with a blouse to put on if it got colder. But now I wasn't so sure. Perhaps I needed to dress up a bit. Deep down, I knew I wanted to make Matt fancy me rather than Cat, but I was hardly admitting it even to myself. I certainly wanted to look nice for him. There wasn't anyone else. So what did I have that was sexy? There was the bikini top and short shiny skirt option. It wasn't quite my style, but it was as near naked as I could get. What if it got cold? I packed a sweatshirt in a backpack, along with a towel, just in case we swam. I wasn't sparing with the make-up. Foundation to hide a couple of spots, a bit of lipstick and a lot of eye-liner. I put my hair in plaits to look trendy and I was all ready bar the shoes. Nothing looked right. The high-heeled strappy sandals looked the best. I tottered downstairs, chucked a couple of cans of coke, a potato and the last frozen veggie-burger in its box into the backpack, along with the sweatshirt and towel, and set off for

Cat's, hoping I could ride pillion in these shoes. But Cat's house was still all dark. No one there. I went back home and rang her mobile number. No reply. I went down to Tanya's. She and Liza had already gone. So I had to go down with my uncle and aunt. I sat in the back of their car and had to endure Uncle Alan's comments on my outfit until Aunty Pat took pity on me and made him be quiet.

Once they'd dropped me I saw Tanya and Liza walking over to the dunes in front of me and took off my shoes to run and catch them up. They were both wearing cargo shorts with sleeveless tops, and flip-flops. They turned as they heard me panting after them.

'Blimey!' said Tanya. 'You look like a townie off to the disco on Friday night.'

'Oh, she doesn't look that bad,' said Liza. 'I like your skirt, Josie. I decided against mine in the end. I thought it maybe made me look a bit tarty. You've got better legs than me, though. I'm sure the boys will be impressed. Just make sure you don't try anything on with my Sebastian.' She peered along the path behind me. 'So what have you done with Cat?'

'She wasn't there. I'm sure she'll be down here soon.' I was determined not to be put off by anything this evening. I knew I looked sexy. The other two didn't understand about fashion. Cat would probably be dressed just like me – we often did the same things without even knowing. 'Hey, look, they've got the bonfire going! Tonight is just going to be *so* fab!'

Seven

We came down from the dunes on to the beach. The bonfire builders had made an area theirs, although there were still plenty of families and dog-walkers around. Everyone was good natured. Somehow you got the feeling that the adults remembered doing this when they were younger and the parents knew their children would do it when they were older – no one seemed to resent the intrusion of a large group of teenagers.

I stood on the edge of the dunes while the other two went ahead. I wanted to assess the situation. I hadn't expected to be here without Cat. I missed her, even though she would have gone off with Matt soon enough.

Seth was hard at work on the bonfire with a couple of other boys. They had amassed a huge pile of driftwood. Blue smoke spiralled up into the sky. The scent of woodsmoke wafted over to where I stood. With the gleaming sea, the wash of waves and the sun slowly dropping, it was all too romantic for words. I looked for our boys. Tanya and Liza had already claimed Paul and Sebastian. They were standing talking in an excited group, though Liza and Sebastian never stay still for long – I saw Liza darting off along the shallows for Sebastian to chase her. Luke and Matt were smoking and chatting to each other, drinking from cans. There were plenty of kids I knew only by sight, including a stunningly beautiful new-agey girl called Bathsheba. She was circling round our group in a predatory way. I thought I'd better keep an eye on Matt, if Cat didn't turn up!

Not wanting to appear as the sad loser who always hovers on the fringes of popular groups, I decided it was time to go and join in. Now, did I want to be with Seth and his hippie friends – it might help to re-establish our relationship (platonic, naturally) – or with Tanya, Liza and the boys? No contest, really. Shoes still in hand, I was drawn as if by a magnet to Matt and the group that surrounded him.

'Hi guys,' I said. In fact, Bathsheba was the only one who answered.

'Hi,' she said. 'Can you introduce me to these people? I've seen you at the pub. You lot always seem to be having a good time. I'm Bathsheba, by the way.'

I was flattered to be considered part of the elite. 'Well—' I started.

'I'm Luke,' said Luke, before I had a chance to introduce her.

'And I'm Matt. Good to meet you, Bathsheba.'

'And I'm Josie,' I added in rather a small voice.

Suddenly Tanya was bellowing in my ear – 'Seth! Hey, Seth! Is that fire hot enough for barbecuing, yet? I'm starving!'

'Thanks for deafening me,' I said.

'Sorry,' she said, 'but I'm so hungry. Fancy coming over to the bonfire with me to find out?'

'OK.' If I stuck with Tanya at least I'd have a good reason to go back to the group. 'Do you want an excuse to get away from Paul or something?'

'No, I'm just hungry, that's all. Come on, let's go and ask Seth.' (Tanya doesn't have problems with Seth.) The bonfire was well under way. 'How's it doing, Seth?' Tanya asked.

'Cool,' said Seth, '– I mean hot. We're ready to roll. You could go and tell people to bring their food.'

'I'll go,' said Tanya. 'You stay with Seth, Josie.' Was she trying to keep me away from Matt? Seth smiled at me, which was a relief after our stand-off.

'You look cool,' he said. 'Tres sexy.'

'Oh, thanks,' I blushed. I definitely hadn't dressed like this for Seth's benefit, but it was nice to be complimented.

'Got a burger or something?' he asked.

I delved into my backpack for the potato and the burger. He put the burger on the barbecue they'd set up and pulled off a bit of tinfoil to wrap my potato in. Very efficient. 'How will I know which potato is mine?'

'I'll know,' Seth said. 'Trust me.' He gave me a glittery grin. 'Do us a favour, Jo-jo?'

'Depends what it is.'

'Sing my song with me? I told a couple of people about it. Said I'd play it later on. And a few of our others? There's another guitar you can play.'

I really did want to be friends with Seth again. 'OK. When?'

'About half an hour, when people are eating?'

'If you think it won't ruin their digestion.'

Seth flipped my burger over. A queue was already forming and he was busy. 'Paper plates over there. Salads over on that rock. Ivan and Tanya's mum did them.' I grabbed a plate and he put the burger on it. 'See you later, then, where the guitars are.' He pointed to another large rock where several guitars and a radio rested on a groundsheet. I carried my food back to the others.

Tanya looked up from where she was sitting with Paul (on his lap, virtually) 'Seth let you go, then?' she said.

'Yes. Why shouldn't he?' I didn't want Matt and co. to think there was anything going on between me and Seth. I say Matt and co. – in fact Paul and Tanya were now being all misty-eyed with one another, Liza and Sebastian had come to rest, literally, and were lying down together – I didn't like to look too hard at what they were up to – and Luke was deep in conversation with Bathsheba. So Matt was the only person likely to benefit from this information anyway. And he didn't look that interested. In fact I almost felt sorry for him without Cat.

I decided to suppress my own feelings for him and go and commiserate. I sat down beside him. 'Want a bit of burger, Matt?'

He actually smiled at me. 'OK, don't mind if I have a nibble. I forgot to bring any food. Thought Cat was going to sort that out.'

'I – I thought she'd be back for this. She was really looking forward to it.'

'So did I. Seems like Daddy from the Dark Ages has won the day.'

'What do you mean?'

'He's managed to keep her away from Evil Matt.'

'You're not evil, Matt. That is so unfair.'

'Isn't it, just.'

I handed over the burger, dripping with ketchup. He took a bite and passed it back, but a bit dropped off and fell down my bikini top. It was still quite hot, and I leapt up, but Matt said, wickedly, 'Sit down. That bit was mine, and I want it.' So I sat down and he hooked out the bit of burger with his finger from where it was lodged and put it in his mouth. 'Mmmm,' he said, licking his finger, and smiled at me, long and slow. I nearly keeled over. 'You should wear more clothes,' he said, and gave my bare shoulder a sly stroke. 'Then accidents wouldn't happen.'

I looked around nervously to see if anyone else had heard this little exchange, but they were all engrossed in each other. Someone waving caught my eye and I was suddenly terrified that it might be Cat, but it wasn't, it was Seth.

'I promised Seth I'd sing,' I said to Matt, forgetting that he didn't know that this was quite a normal occurrence.

'Suit yourself,' he said. 'Perhaps I'll catch you later if Cat doesn't show.'

'OK,' I said, running off, and it was a while before I registered his words. Matt was going to 'catch' me – if Cat didn't turn up! Perversely I prayed that Cat was all right. I couldn't bear the thought that the power of my wishes had somehow put her out of action. It was all too scary.

Seth handed me a guitar. He'd spread a blanket on the sand near the fire for us and people were sitting round expectantly. I raised my eyes to where I'd been, and saw that even my lot were waiting for something to happen. I tried not to focus on where Matt was sitting. His lazy smile and deft touch were still with me.

Seth and I should have practised more, but we managed to play for nearly half an hour. Our voices worked really well together, and I concentrated on playing the guitar to take my mind off Matt. Even Seth's latest composition, the 'sweet soft smile' one, sounded good in that setting. I sang it on my own, and caught Seth's eye as we were finishing. He motioned for us to do a repeat, so we sang it again and he put in some really excellent harmonies. Everyone clapped when it came to an end.

'Thanks, Jo-jo,' said Seth, punching my arm as I put the guitar down. 'Thanks mate, that was cool.' He quickly turned on the radio which was tuned to Latino FM and everyone came down to join in the dirty dancing. Seth retired to talk to some friends. *Some friends?* It was the dolphin boys! I hadn't seen them earlier, but they seemed to be congratulating Seth. I'd forgotten he knew them. But then everything went from my mind because someone had their hands on my behind and was dancing with me – Matt!

'Yeah, well,' he said, when I glanced at him questioningly, and went into a pretty fair version of the salsa. I can salsa – Holly and I went to classes – but it's hard, and most boys I know can't get into the rhythm of it at all. They waggle their shoulders and not their hips. Not Matt.

WOW! Was I happy! Gloriously happy. I was on the beach, with *my* crowd, dancing with Matt. I hooked my arms around his neck and he slid his hands round to my hips. I felt very naked indeed as his warm breath lapped my ear. 'You can certainly dance,' he murmured, and moved my hips in time with his.

The dancing was getting pretty riotous. I let Matt guide me away from the crowd. 'Perhaps we should find a bit of privacy,' he said, and edged me further round the beach. We climbed up a little and found a patch of soft sand and tussocky grass. I could hear the waves, but not see them. The music was just a distant beat. I lay back next to Matt. As the sun set over the dunes I closed my eyes and waited for the inevitable kiss.

But Matt wasn't so hasty. He kissed my eyelids and stroked my face. He ran his thumb over my lips and teeth tantalisingly (except I died a thousand times thinking it was because he couldn't bring himself to kiss my train tracks) until I tried to bite it, and only then did he bring his mouth down on mine. With passion. Crikey. This was serious stuff and it was wonderful. Matt and me – I couldn't believe my dreams had come true as he pressed the full weight of his warm flesh against me.

'Josie! Josie?' Two girls were calling out my name as they descended on our hiding place. Tanya and Liza. 'I thought I saw her go off in this direction.'

'So did I. I saw her shiny skirt.'

'Was she with a bloke?'

'I think so, but I didn't see who.' She called again. 'Josie?'

Matt swore quietly. 'Do yourself up,' he whispered. 'And here, have my T-shirt.'

'It's OK,' I whispered back. 'I've got a sweatshirt in my bag here.' I put it on.

'I think we'd better pretend this didn't happen, don't you?' Matt said, as the voices got closer.

'OK,' I said, feeling hurt, but knowing it was for the best. I stood up and waved. 'Hi you two!' I called. 'I'm up here. With Matt. We went for a walk. We were talking about Cat,' I added, for authenticity.

'Well, your dad's looking for you,' said Tanya.'

'Oh no, not another dad on the warpath,' groaned Matt quietly.

'I thought my uncle was fetching me. Oh well. Better go back then,' I said, determined to stay cool. I climbed down. Matt ran down the slope behind me, digging his heels into the sand.

'So what have you done with my mates?' he said to the girls. 'I thought they were going to take you back to the campsite?'

'No way!' said Tanya and Liza sanctimoniously, and I didn't know whether to feel smug or terrible. As it was, I was far too worried about Dad's reaction to me going missing.

As we came back round the beach I heard music again. Not the radio, but someone playing rock and roll. It was pretty dark, but I could make out figures hunched over guitars by the bonfire. One or two people were listening, but most had drifted off. We went up closer. Someone was singing 'Hey Jude' – badly, but with feeling. The other guitarist had something glinting in his ear. No wonder everyone had disappeared. The artistes in question were my dad and Ivan. I could have died.

'Oh God,' said Tanya. 'My brother. How embarrassing.' Then she looked at me pityingly. 'But not half as bad as your dad!' she said as Paul and Sebastian turned up to stare at the awful spectacle.

Matt was right behind me. I so much wanted to reach back and take his hand, but I didn't dare. As we both

77

stood, mesmerised by this terrible performance, Dad put on a pair of swimming goggles that he'd found and started on the Na na na nana na na's in a falsetto voice, before grabbing Ivan and waltzing him round the bonfire. I stepped back. 'I'm really sorry you had to see that,' I said to Matt, mortified.

I had to stop Dad and the only way to stop him was to make my presence known and offer myself up for the lift home. 'Bye Matt,' I said, and gave him a peck on the cheek. He caught me and kissed me on the mouth, in front of everyone. 'You're sweet,' he said. 'But this is all it was, OK?' and he turned to the others and led their retreat.

I gulped and stepped towards the fire. 'Dad! I'm here!' I thought I might as well lay it on thick. 'Good guitar playing!'

He removed the goggles and tossed them back to where he'd found them. 'Thank you. I enjoyed that. Now, got your gear? And where's Seth? Alan and Pat are waiting in the bar to take us all home.'

Seth stepped from the shadows. He spoke to the dolphin boys who were staying by the fire. (I still couldn't get used to the idea that dear old Seth was on speaking terms with such cool guys. Everyone else I knew was rather in awe of them.) He picked up his guitar and his skateboard but he didn't speak to me. People were threading their way through the sand dunes along the little paths. It was dark now. As the paths converged I overheard little snippets of conversation. I was pretty disgusted by what I heard. 'I'm glad my dad doesn't make a tit of himself in front of my friends . . .' 'Matt, you jammy so-and-so – you didn't, did you? That'll up your score.' 'Not as such. But no one's to tell the other one . . .' 'Luke's bird's a goer – I reckon he'll get more points than me.'

I hurried on, sticking close behind Dad. Seth followed. He was still silent. My uncle and aunt were waiting outside the pub for us. 'Well, that seemed to be a jolly little do,' said Dad. 'I reckon we'd have had a wilder time in our day, Alan!' (Hypocrite) 'But you enjoyed your-selves, didn't you, kids?'

'Josie obviously did,' said Seth, glowering at me.

I climbed into the back of the car with him. Aunty Pat was leaning forward to talk to my dad. 'What's the matter, Seth?' I asked. 'We were great!'

'Exactly,' said Seth. 'And then you had to go and spoil it.'

I looked at him. This wasn't fair. 'What did I spoil?'

Seth didn't reply. But after a while he said petulantly, 'And you never came back for your potato. I was guarding it for you.'

This had to be so ridiculous. I was about to round on him for being babyish but from the way Seth was humming and jigging his legs I judged I'd better keep quiet. When we got home he grabbed his things and took off up the hill without saying goodbye.

I went straight up to bed too. I needed to be on my own. A quick glance in the mirror reminded me how messed up my make-up was – thank goodness it had been dusk on the beach. But I didn't want to look too hard in the mirror right now. I wanted to forget Seth, forget what I'd overheard. I just wanted to dive into bed and relive my time with Matt.

I lay there in the dark for a while, clutching Monk.

Matt had been dead sexy. We hadn't – you know – or anything, but he'd been pretty passionate. And he'd kissed my eyelids! That was so gentle and so sweet! But there was no one I could share it with. That was the irony. I'd just got off with the most popular boy in Cornwall and I couldn't tell anyone. If only Cat hadn't got there first. It seemed so unfair. Everyone would have liked me so much more if they'd seen how attractive Matt found me.

I sat up and switched on the light. Part of my brain was singing 'I got off with Matt. I got off with Matt,' but another part was asking, 'What about Cat? What about Cat?' I could sort of justify it. After all, I really did fancy Matt, and he must have fancied me at least a little bit. And Cat had been funny about him lately.

And then I did one of those awful, horrified intakes of breath. 'Oh no!' What if Cat found out somehow? What if anyone found out? I mean, everyone would know about the very public kiss on the beach because Matt had done that intentionally, so that he could say, yes, I gave her a quick kiss, but everyone saw it and there was nothing to it. Quite cunning really. I suppose he could even say it was because I was Cat's friend. But what if they found out that we'd gone a bit further than that? Cat would kill me. But no one knew, did they? Would Matt tell anyone? *'Matt, you jammy so-and-so, you didn't, did you?'* Matt already *had* told someone.

I wrote a quick and very private list that included quite a few things you *can* do with a fixed brace. Then I put out the light and tried to dream about Matt and not think about tomorrow. I was just dropping off when I heard a car pulling up outside Cat's cottage, followed by the voices of Cat and her parents as they made their way indoors, though I couldn't make out what they were saying.

What had I done?

Eight

I didn't sleep brilliantly. I woke up at some unearthly hour – the rooster down the road was making a racket – and wrote another list to try and sort things out:

Best case scenario
Matt to finish with Cat and her not to mind.
Matt to start going out with me.
Cat to go out with one of the others, perhaps Luke.
Cat only to hear about the public kiss and not mind.
For us to be a cool eightsome.
Seth to just be friends again.

Worst case scenario
Cat to hear about me getting off with Matt.
Cat to mind terribly.
Cat to hate me.
Cat to make everyone else hate me, including Matt.
Seth to hate me.

The best-case scenario was slightly over optimistic. I did another more realistic one:

Most likely best case scenario
Cat hears about public kiss and doesn't mind much.
Cat carries on going out with Matt.
Matt blanks me and pretends nothing happened.
Seth goes back to being my friend.

Hmm. Since the first best scenario was pretty unlikely, the future looked bleak. It all depended on who knew what, and I needed to find that out as soon as possible. I finally fell asleep again and woke to hear small cousins thundering up and down the stairs, probably with the express purpose of torturing me. I threw on some clothes and tottered down to breakfast.

'Good *morning*, big sister!' said Tim, looking far too bright for the early hour. Oh God, what did *he* know?

'Harrumph.' I tipped coco-pops into my bowl.

'Gather you and Dad and Ivan entertained the troops last night.'

'Shut up. I thought you might come. Where were you?'

'Sailing with Harry and Archie. Much more fun. Hey, guess what?'

'I don't know. What?'

Tim moved closer. 'Harry and I are going to Newquay today.'

'Oh yeah?' I failed to see the significance of that. Dad came in, still in his dressing-gown. I think he'd over-done it somewhat in the pub. Time to get my own back. 'Oh God, it's the rock and roll star. Morning, Dad.'

'What about this singing then, Jo-jo?'

'You were embarrassing, Dad. I can say that in the cold light of day.'

'I didn't mean last night. The DIY oratorio. It starts this evening. We'll have Nicholas Elliott conducting us!'

Now that was pretty amazing. For those not in the know, Nicholas Elliott conducts the last night of the proms sometimes. It would definitely be something to hit my muso friends with. Even my favourite drummer would be impressed. But no. Singing in a choir on holiday was too deeply sad and tragic.

'Sorry, Dad. No go. I'm doing a painting, for heaven's sake. Some people are never satisfied.'

'Oh well,' Dad sighed. 'How about clocking up some brownie points by popping down to the shop for some milk and a paper. Your cousins seem to have had a cereal feast judging by the state of the table. They've all gone off to the beach. I told Mum we'd join them later.'

I was going to tell him to ask Tim, if he was that desperate, but then I reconsidered. If I went out I could call on Tanya or Liza and test the water a bit. 'OK, Dad. Give me some money then.'

I glanced up at Cat's cottage, and Seth's beyond that. The sound of children's voices drifted down from Seth's, but in Cat's the curtains were still drawn. The car was there though. I carried on down the hill. I thought I'd go to the shop first – it would take a bit of courage to call in on Tanya or Liza. Such a shame when in other circum-stances my friends would have rallied round to con-gratulate me. I wished I could phone Holly, but she wasn't at home. She was staying with her new boyfriend in the country. I wondered how she was getting on. Holly wouldn't get off with her best friend's boyfriend, would she? We just wouldn't do that to each other. So was Cat a different sort of best friend?

I pushed open the shop door. As it clanged to, that lovely village shop smell washed over me – sweets and newspapers and an undertone of talcum powder. I gathered up a big plastic bottle of milk and queued to collect our paper. The door clanged again, and Tanya and Liza came in. 'Hi!' I called, waving.

I waited while they went round the shelf unit that ran down the centre of the shop. They reappeared with baskets of shopping and stood behind me in the queue. 'Hi, you two,' I said again.

At first they didn't reply.

Then Tanya came up to me and hissed, 'We don't associate with people like you.'

I stared at them both, at a loss for words.

'And I wouldn't like to be in your shoes when Cat gets to hear about it.'

I tried to summon some sense of righteousness. 'It was only a friendly kiss,' I said, making light of it.

'Oh yeah,' said Tanya. 'We're not stupid, Josie. Matt doesn't exactly drag girls off into the dunes for a *chat*, now, does he?'

I paid for my paper and milk. I wanted to go. But Tanya had more to say. 'Just because Luke preferred Bathsheba, you thought you'd go for Matt instead, didn't you? As soon as Cat's back was turned! Never mind that he's already spoken for.'

I'd had enough. 'Oh shut up, Tanya. You don't know anything!' Suddenly all those snippets of the boys' conversation added up – about points and scores and winners. They were having a competition! And we were their willing victims! I wanted Tanya and Liza to feel as bad as I did. 'I never fancied Luke anyway. All four of those boys are only in it for a competition – a bet! They're notching us up. And Matt's winning – in one department. But in fact, Luke's winning because Bathsheba is a bit freer with her favours than you two are. So there!'

I marched off. I'd scored a few points, but I can't say I was happy. Liza hadn't said a word. And I was dreading meeting Cat.

I dumped the stuff on the kitchen table. 'I'm going to work on my picture, Dad. And I'm having more positive thoughts about the singing. Try me again this afternoon. The Nicholas Elliott factor might just win me over.'

Dad smiled. 'That's my girl,' he said. I went over and gave him a hug. At least in Dad's eyes I could be perfect.

I set myself up in the window of my bedroom, kneeling on the floor with the paper on the broad window-seat. I had a board to rest on and a good selection of materials to work with. I pulled out my sketches. I'd gone off the idea of a boy morphing into a dolphin. Better just to have a boy with the dolphins, almost indistinguishable from them. I did some sketches of a boy with his arms pointed over his head as if diving, and flippers on his feet. It was possible to make him into a dolphin shape. I drew loads of them. I imagined the scene from just below the water's surface. The sky would be pearly with dawn or sunset, perhaps some smoke up there too, from a bonfire on the beach. And this boy, he was joining in the playing and leaping. He didn't want to be human any more – he wanted to lose his human form – he simply wanted the freedom to *be*.

I worked away for ages. There was a diminishing pattern of dolphins, like an underwater dance, and then there were three bursting out of the water, with the water breaking up in the light. And if you looked really hard you would see that in fact one of the three was a boy. It was hard to make out his features, but in my head it was the younger dolphin boy, the one who'd caught my eye on the ferry. (I mean, it was sort of me, too – you probably gathered that – but right then I wasn't quite sure precisely *what* I was expressing, I just knew I needed to express it.)

The hours slipped by. Tim put his head round the door to say he was off to Newquay with Harry. They'd worked it all out and Harry was dead excited. He plucked at his earlobe. 'Watch this space,' he said.

'Tim! They'll murder you!'

'Why should they? You had yours done.'

'Suppose so.'

Tim saw what I was doing and came over to look. 'Honestly, Jo-jo,' he said, and I braced myself for the insults. 'You spend ninety per cent of the time acting like a total bimbo and then you go and produce stuff like this. It's going to be brilliant. I'll never understand women, not even my own sister.'

He went off to Newquay. It had been a backhanded compliment of a sort.

Then Dad came up. 'Do you want to come to the beach with me?'

'No thanks, Dad. I'm doing this.'

'And what's "this"?' He came over to the window. 'You're a clever little thing, Jo-jo, you really are. You must show Grandma this some time. She'll be thrilled.'

(My grandad who died last year was quite a well known artist. I used to paint with him when I was little.) 'Well, you stay here and work on it by all means. I can see quite a big price sticker going on this.'

I'd forgotten that. Dad went off, and I wondered just how much I might get for it. Ten quid would come in very handy right now. I made myself a sandwich and started colouring. I laid down a mauvey watercolour wash to start with. I'd collected a few shells during the week and I crushed them into the colour I was using for a bit of sparkle. It was coming along nicely. As I painted I thought of me and Matt in the dunes once or twice, but I put the memories away and concentrated on working. It was the best cure, it really was. If Cat had come by on her bike or Seth on his skateboard, I hadn't heard them.

At six o'clock Tim came back with Harry. They came upstairs to find me. They were extremely pleased with themselves. 'Look!' they cried, both displaying rather red ears with a little gold hoop in.

'Tim squealed,' said Harry proudly. 'But I didn't.'

'Harry wants a haircut, now, Josie,' said Tim. 'I said you'd do it for him.'

'What, now? Can't you see I'm busy?'

'Well, you're not going to finish that tonight if you go off singing. Go on, Josie!'

'I want to give my parents the fright of their lives,' said Harry, beaming.

'But—' I looked at dear straight old Harry. I wasn't sure *I* wanted him different. 'Couldn't you just style it differently? Lose the parting? You could do that for him, Tim. I've got to finish this for Sunday whatever happens.'

'Oh, OK,' said Tim. 'Come into the bathroom Harry. I might snip a bit off for you. I think I know what to do.'

'Cool!' said Harry, and they left me in peace.

But not for long. I think it was deliberate. A few minutes later, Tim pushed Harry in at the door. 'Josie! Oh look what I've done!' And there was Harry with great chunks chopped out of his hair. It was long on one side and short on the other.

I heaved a sigh and followed them back to the bathroom. 'One thing,' I said severely. 'I didn't do this, OK? You had it done at the hairdresser's. I'm in enough trouble already and I don't want your parents blaming me for ruining their precious little Harry.'

'Were you caught down the pub again, Josie?' asked Harry as I tucked a towel round him.

'Far worse than that!' said Tim. 'She was caught *in flagrante* with Cat's boyfriend!'

I spun round, scissors in hand, and nearly took his eye out. 'What? Is that the story that's going round?'

'It's true, isn't it?'

I started snipping Harry's hair. 'Only sort of,' I said. 'Matt started it. He came up and danced with me and then – led me away.'

'Led you astray by the sound of it,' said Tim.

'That,' I said, 'is none of your business. He – kissed me, that's all.'

'So what were you up to when Tanya found you both? Ivan says you were—'

'No one knows what we were doing because no one was there. I told Tanya we were talking about Cat. Anything else is the result of her fevered imagination.' It was true. No one had seen us, I knew that. And it gave me a bit of hope. I could simply deny that anything had happened. We had been alone. It had been between Matt and me. He started it. I fancied him, so I went along with it. Anyone would have. It was hard enough for me that it wasn't going to carry on, without everyone giving me grief.

'Ow!' I'd snipped Harry's other ear, the non-pierced one. It was time to concentrate.

'Pass me Dad's electric razor, Tim.'

By the time I'd finished, Harry really was transformed. The short hair suited him. Showed off his navy-blue eyes as well as the earring and the sore ears. 'Cool!' he said, over and again, when he looked at himself in the mirror.

'My pleasure,' I said. 'You two clear up, and mind you make a good job of it. The parents will be back any minute now.'

The church is tiny and ancient and beautiful. At this time of year it's like a little boat sailing on a golden sea of cornfields. Nicholas Elliott was already there organising people into voices. Dad and Ivan are tenors. I'm an alto. He organised us so the tenors stood behind the sopranos and the basses stood behind the altos. As I picked up my music and went to my place, Nicholas said, 'Good, you must be the lass. I'd like a word with you later.'

I didn't have time to wonder why because we started straight into the Haydn, sight-reading it. Then we had a short break and whizzed through the Handel. Nicholas knew exactly what he wanted out of us, but this was just a taster. By the end of the weekend we'd sound professional. There were a few songs included in the programme. One had apparently been written especially for us, something Cornish and evocative, Nicholas said.

We were just gathering up the music at the end when two boys came down the aisle towards us. Gideon and Caleb! 'Well, thank you very much for deigning to turn up, boys,' said Nicholas.

'Sorry Dad,' said the older dolphin boy. 'Big drama on the beach. One of the surfers we know had an accident. Did something stupid over on Breakneck Rocks. Nearly drowned.'

'But he's OK,' said the younger one. 'Just staying overnight in hospital. Didn't you hear the helicopter?'

I saw Ivan prick up his ears. He went over to the boys. 'Who was it? Who was it?' he asked. 'Was it anyone I know?'

'Guy called Matt,' said the older dolphin boy. 'You know him, don't you?' He was looking at me.

My heart was in my knees somewhere. 'But he's OK, isn't he?'

'Yeah, fine,' said the younger one, looking at me with his sea-grey eyes. 'Now have you talked to Dad about the song?'

'Not yet she hasn't,' said Nicholas to him. 'Can you give me five minutes, dear, just while I sort this music out?'

'Of course,' I said.

I nipped outside to one of my favourite places in the world – the part of the graveyard with a view over the fields to the sea – and leant against a headstone. It was all a bit too much to take in. Vying for space in my brain were the major items of news:

1 Matt was in hospital
2 The dolphin boys were Nicholas Elliott's sons – and
   they knew who I was!

All this quite apart from the traumas of last night (Matt)
and today (Tanya and Liza, not to mention the rest of
the world).

I stood there, letting the tranquil evening wash over
me. My life was far too complicated for me even to
attempt to untangle it. Matt wasn't dead or anything.
But I was about to have an interview with a very famous
conductor.

I took a few deep breaths and went back into the
church. Dad was in the porch with Ivan. 'Oh, there you
are,' Dad said. 'Thought we'd lost you.'

'Worried about Matt, are you?' said Ivan, a touch
sneakily.

I ignored him. 'Nicholas Elliott wants to talk to me,
Dad. Don't know why. I'll be out again in five minutes.
See you in the car?'

Nicholas was down at the front of the church. I
suddenly felt dreadfully in awe of him. 'Ah, Jo – is it?
Giddy wasn't altogether sure that that was your name.'

'Yes,' I said, brain still reeling. 'Jo is fine.'

He carried on sifting through piles of music as he
spoke. 'We need the voice of a very young woman for
this Max Barnes song. Raw and inexperienced. Innocent. It's about the Annunication, you see. He wants us
to imagine Mary, terrified and overawed. But she's
pierced to the heart by love, you see – for God, for the
angel, for her unborn child.' (Nicholas Elliott talked like
that.) 'I was going to do auditions, but there aren't many

91

teenage girls here, and Giddy's heard you sing. Says you'd be perfect. How would you feel?'

'Is – is it very exposed?'

'No. That's the thing. It's accompanied by woodwind and cello. They weave in and out. The voice is mostly another instrument. It's a lovely piece. Quite folky and haunting. Have you ever sung or played in an ensemble?'

'Yes. I'm a clarinettist – or was until this thing.' I pointed at my brace. 'But I sing and play the guitar.'

'Talented girl.'

'Not really.'

'Well, it's late and I have to be getting home. Unfortunately I've forgotten the music. Stupid of me.' He tapped his forehead while he thought. 'Did you come here in a car?'

'Yes. With my dad.'

'Then perhaps you could drop me off at my house and I'll hand it over. We're only a few hundred yards down the lane.'

We went out into the car park, past the church hall where the art exhibition was to be held. Dad was standing on tiptoe trying to peer in the window. He heard me approaching, and spoke without turning his head. 'So what did the great man want with my little Josie?'

'To sing one of our songs,' said Nicholas to his back. 'And she's kindly offered me a lift home so she can pick up the music. I hope that's all right by you.'

Poor Dad did a wonderful double-take. 'Good grief! Yes, of course.' He opened the car door. 'Into the back, Ivan. I think we'll let Nicholas Elliott sit in the front seat, don't you?'

When we reached the Elliott's house I got out with the conductor. The younger son opened their front door to us. 'Whatcha, Gids,' his father said, thus answering my question as to which brother was Caleb and which was Gideon. Nicholas turned to me. 'Come in, young lady, come in.' He called to his wife in the kitchen. 'Eileen, I think we've found our Virgin at last! Can you lay your hands on the music?' I stood there nervously, not daring to catch Gideon's eye. Did his father have to put it like that?

Caleb bounced down the stairs. 'Is Gideon's Virgin here?' he called. I nearly died. Then he ducked round the corner and saw me. 'Of course. I hadn't made the connection. You're the one that was with the guy who had the accident! And you're Gideon's Virgin! One and the same. Well, well.'

I took the pages of music, thanked Nicholas, and ran out of the door. Today had been altogether too much.

Nine

I found solace in my painting.

It was half past ten by the time Dad and I got in. Tim was in trouble about the ear-piercing, particularly because Harry's parents had been really upset. Tim had already gone to bed, but Mum wanted to discuss the whole business with Dad. So I made my excuses and left. I put my head round Tim's door but he didn't wake up. If he'd spent the evening rowing with Mum, it was quite likely he hadn't picked up any gossip about the accident anyway. What I really wanted to do was pop round to Cat's, but that seemed so impossible now.

The paintings had to be on display for the interval of the concert on Sunday evening, so people could look at them while they had a glass of wine or whatever. They were numbered but not named, and people wrote down what they were prepared to pay. Then the exhibition stayed up for a few days and the pictures went to the highest bidders and the money went to the artists, with ten per cent for the church roof fund. The children's art was sold in the same way – usually parents buy their own children's pictures – but it's quite a good way of fund-raising.

So. It was now late on Friday night. Tomorrow the rehearsal would run from eleven until one; break for lunch; and then from two until four plus a bit of time for extras, like Barnes's 'Annunciation'. I had tomorrow morning and evening (great way to spend Saturday night) and Sunday morning to finish the picture. I set it up and worked on sketching in the leaping dolphins for a bit. I still wasn't quite sure which one was going to be the boy. And then, with a slip of the pencil it was as if I'd given one of them bigger eyes, and hair. It was a sign. I made that one the boy, roughed in the rest of the face. And suddenly – it looked like Gideon. Weird. Somehow I'd made it look like Gideon. It would have made more sense if it had turned out like Matt.

Definitely time for bed!

I spent a long time in front of the mirror taking off my

make-up. I wasn't sure who I was any more. I was lots of people:

1 *Sisterly sort of person to Tim, Harry – maybe Ivan and Seth, too.*
2 *Scarlet woman to Tanya and Liza.*
3 *One-time friend to Cat.*
4 *Silly girl with brace, not much good at anything, e.g. surfing.*
5 *Muso*
6 *Daughter not to be trusted, but OK at painting.*
7 *Gideon's Virgin.*

OK. I know everyone pretends they're not (a virgin, that is), but most of my friends are waiting for someone really, really special to come along. Anyway, that had nothing to do with how I felt about my latest persona as 'Gideon's Virgin'. Hideous embarrassment aside, I was excited by the realisation that Caleb and Gideon and Nicholas Elliott had referred to me like that before they knew my name. And it was because they thought I was good at something. And, compared to all the other Josies, 'Gideon's Virgin' was a clean slate, full of potential. 'Jo' in fact. And I'd hardly even spoken to Gideon! Just seen him from a distance, gazing out to sea. Why did he and Caleb do that gazing thing? What were they looking for?

I snuggled down to sleep. All the stuff with Matt seemed a long time ago. (Certainly not like just last night!) I hated the thought of him having an accident, but the way he'd cut me off had hardened me some-what, not to mention their points system, and I wasn't as worried for him as I might have been. I couldn't quite see him welcoming me with open arms at his hospital bedside.

As for Cat – I decided that honesty was going to be the best policy with her. Perhaps I should just tell it how it was: Yes, I had fancied Matt and he'd been very happy to take advantage of that fact while she was away. She had let him down by not turning up, hadn't she? They both had mobiles. She could have called him.

Tim burst into my room. 'Morning Big Sister! Hey, did your ear hurt the next day?'

'Yup. Went yukky, too. You'll need some surgical spirit.'

'My little pierced ear is nothing compared to what happened to your Matt. Ivan told me about it this morning.'

'Not *my* Matt, as you must have gathered. Cat's Matt.'

'His parents are taking him home today, so he's not anyone's Matt. But it was a big emergency. Helicopter and everything.'

'What happened?'

'Tanya found out that the four of them have some long-running competition.' (Bet she didn't say it was from me.) 'You know, points for girls pulled, daring feats, drinking, eating and stuff. Apparently they were level-pegging by yesterday afternoon, and the surf was up, so they decided to ride this really dodgy bit – Breakneck Rock.'

'That's what I heard from Caleb.'

'Matt was the last to go – and he lost it. Went under. As soon as he didn't surface, one of the others called the emergency services. They turned up almost straight away and managed to fish him out. He'd hit his head.'

'Yeah, Caleb said—'

'Hang on! How do you know Caleb? He's a surfer. So's his brother. Aren't they a bit out of your league?'

'Thanks very much. In fact, they're so far out of my league they're singing in the choir.'

'Get away!'

'Their dad is Nicholas Elliott, the conductor.'

'Just shows, doesn't it, how deceptive looks can be. I'd never've had those two down as musos.'

'All right, big head. Harry's parents are none too happy about the new-look Harry, a little bird told me.'

'They'll get used to it.' Tim twiddled the gold hoop in his ear. 'Ooh. Ouch. I wonder if he's suffering as much as I am.'

'I expect so. What are you doing today, while I sing my heart out?'

'The usual. Down to the beach. What's up with Liza and Tanya, by the way? They were dead snotty with me.'

'That'll be because you're my brother, and I committed an unforgivable sin.'

'Is this about you getting off with Matt?' He giggled.

'Yes. Stop laughing! Why are you laughing?'

'All those Cat sat on the Matt jokes. And—'

'And what?'

'Oh, I dunno. It's just that they think they're so cool, those guys. And Liza and Tanya and Cat think they're so cool to be going out with them.'

'They *are* cool, thank you very much. Anyway, what would you know? Red-ears!' I lunged at him and he scampered out of my room.

He made me feel a bit better, though. No one could deny that Cat is cool, but Tanya?

I had three hours until the rehearsal. I decided to devote two of them to the painting, even though part of me was desperate to get the Cat/Matt situation sorted. I worked on all the greys in the sea, remembering the colour of Gideon's eyes as I painted. Then I spent time on the sparkle as the dolphins broke through the waves. I used a bit of glittery make-up for that! It was all blocked in now, and nearly finished, but I needed to spend more time on the figures. I'd have to do that after the rehearsals tonight. Aagh! The Barnes 'Annunciation'! I shot downstairs to find Dad. 'Dad, could you just plunk this through with me on the guitar?'

'Of course. I sometimes wish, oh daughter of mine, that you realised what a little bundle of talent you are.'

'Oh Dad. All parents are programmed to think that. I'm useless at most things. Have you ever seen me try to stand up on a surf board? Come on. It's in C minor.'

We ran through the song. It was really beautiful. It starts off with a sort of splash – that's the angel arriving. But then the angel's words are all soothing – the cello actually plays them. Then the Virgin comes in, all breathless and frightened. First she's overawed by the responsibility but then finally she's overcome by love. Barnes lives in Cornwall and he'd seen paintings of Our Lady of the Sea in a local church – so it inspired him to think of the angel as the waves, or something. I guess I'll just have to bone up on the programme notes! The other thing was that he reckoned Mary was only fourteen or so, which is why he wanted a young voice. It's not a difficult piece, luckily. I'm quite looking forward to it, sad person that I am!

I looked at my watch. Ten-thirty am. I decided to bite the bullet and call in on Cat. I was going to say that whatever she'd heard was probably only partially true, but that I was sorry, and how was Matt? I ran up the path. Seth was coming down. 'Hi Seth!' I ventured. He simply carried on. Great.

I knocked on Cat's door. Her mother answered. She wasn't any use. 'Oh, I hear you're in the concert on Sunday dear. I do wish we could persuade Catherine to do something like that.' Not what I wanted to hear. 'Catherine?' She called up the stairs.

'Who is it?' came Cat's voice.

'Josephine.'

'Well you can tell her to bog off, for a start.'

'I'm so sorry dear,' said her mother.

Oh well. I turned and left. There were Tanya and Liza coming towards me. Liza was about to say something but Tanya stopped her and they both blanked me. I wanted to ask all sorts of questions about the boys and Matt's accident, but I decided to save my breath. I felt like crying, though.

And as soon as I got indoors I ran up to my room and burst into tears. I hauled Monk out from under my duvet and soon his fur was soaking wet. I knew I'd behaved badly with Matt, but – well, no excuses, it was bad. No wonder they didn't like me. Dad knocked on the door while I was putting on make-up to try and hide the fact that I'd been bawling. 'Coming, Dad.' I had to feel a bit glad I was doing the singing – I wasn't sure what I'd be doing otherwise right now.

The church was lovely and cheerful in the morning sun. There were pools of coloured light on the floor from the stained glass and it felt bright and airy. We started with the Handel this time. Caleb and Gideon are both basses, so they were standing in the row behind me. I could hear them booming away, Caleb particularly, as he's older and his voice is fuller. I felt shy of them, especially after what Tim had said about them being out of my league. I talked to Dad and Ivan in the coffee break. We spent the rest of the morning on the Handel – it was beginning to sound great. I love Handel anyway – it's always so sort of *jubilant*! You can't feel gloomy if you're singing Handel.

Dad and I whizzed home for lunch, dropping Ivan off on the way. Ivan was still being creepy, but he was up-to-date with the latest gossip from Tanya. He knew I was a social outcast, but I think he felt he had some sort of diplomatic immunity in our car. He told me that apparently Cat had missed the barbecue because they'd gone to visit relations and couldn't get away. (I still think she should have phoned Matt.) But she hadn't exactly hurried to see him yesterday, and that, Ivan informed me, was *before* Tanya and Liza had given her the news about Matt and me – or *'told her what you'd done'* was how he put it. Cat had been put in the picture around lunchtime and then all three girls had gone down to the surfing beach to meet up with the boys, Cat primed to forgive Matt and excommunicate me. Obviously Ivan couldn't tell me what had gone on between

Cat and Matt, but anyway it wasn't long before the boys decided to go for the Breakneck Rock competition (to sort out those extra points, I guessed). Then Matt had had his accident.

We arrived outside Ivan and Tanya's cottage at this point and dropped him off for lunch. I was determined to catch up with any further developments on the way back.

Which were as follows: the girls had spent yesterday evening at Tanya's house slagging me off. (Thanks Ivan.) Then the six of them had gone to visit Matt in hospital this morning. He'd had an incredibly lucky escape, but his parents were definitely taking him home. Luke's parents were also pressing for the boys to spend the rest of their holiday with them. Matt's accident had put the wind up everybody. So now it seemed as if Tanya and Liza and Cat were all going to be without boyfriends, and apparently it was all my fault. Great.

I felt pretty wretched as we went back into the church for the afternoon rehearsal. Scared too, about the Barnes 'Annunication' later on. The Haydn was difficult and Nicholas Elliott was getting frustrated with us. I sensed his sons' discomfort from the row behind and wondered why on earth I was subjecting myself to this on my holiday. But towards the end of the afternoon, we got some of it right, and it was such a fabulous sound as the harmonies soared up to the roof that I remembered why I did it.

Then everybody left and it was time to rehearse the Barnes.

I say I was nervous, but the singing in itself doesn't actually bother me. I open my mouth and I know I can sing in tune, so it feels – well, natural. Nicholas didn't have the musicians there, so he had to accompany me himself on the church organ! I followed him up to the organ loft. It sounded gorgeous and echoey in the church – like singing in the bath. It was quite good, because I did start off a bit nervous and in awe (of Nicholas Elliott), but then I felt I could let rip because it sounded so nice. We went back over some of the harder bits, but I could tell he was pleased with me. 'Well done, Jo,' he said. 'Now, I've got the players coming over to my house this evening. Could you possibly spare the time to come along? No barbecues to miss tonight, eh?'

I had been going to finish my painting, but I supposed there'd be time for both. 'I have got something else to do later. Might we be finished by half-past nine?'

'Oh yes. My Gideon's playing the cello, and he'll want to be off and out by then too.'

We went down into the church. Gideon and Caleb sat sprawled in the pews. 'You're very good,' Caleb volunteered.

'Don't sound so surprised,' said Gideon. 'I *said* she was good.'

'OK, you two, don't embarrass the poor girl or she'll change her mind about rehearsing tonight,' said Nicholas.

Dad and Ivan appeared from the back of the church. Dad's eyes were glistening slightly. Oh God. He always cries when I perform. What d'you do? Ivan started telling me more about the girls hating me on the way back, but I'd suddenly had enough. 'Ivan, shut up. I don't need this. OK. I screwed up. End of story. Maybe Cat will have forgiven me by next year. Maybe she won't. Quite frankly I don't care if I never speak to your sister again. Maybe I'll just go somewhere else for my holidays. Meanwhile I've got a scary solo to worry about.'

Ivan did shut up. Then he said, 'By the way, you've got a great voice,' and got out.

'Might I ask what's going on?' asked Dad as we walked up the long front path.

'No,' I said. It was half past five. The Barnes rehearsal was at eight and it would take twenty minutes or so to get there. I had to get on with the painting. After tonight there would only be a couple of hours in the morning. Dad had bought one of those clip frames for it already.

The cottage was full of idiotic boys. Tim and the cousins were playing another mad card game with Harry and Archie and Seth. I saw Seth about to slip off, but I was still feeling bullish.

I went up to him. 'Seth – I want to talk to you.' He started to look away and ignore me, but I wasn't having it. 'Now,' I said. 'In my room.' Seth looked hunted but I made him go up the stairs in front of me so he couldn't escape. I sat him on the bed. 'OK. Now I know I wasn't too pleasant the other night, but since then we've made friends *and* I sang with you when you asked me, so what's the matter now? It's bad enough that Tanya and Liza are punishing me, but I'm not having you being so childish.' Seth wouldn't look me in the eye. 'Go on,' I said.

'Liza and Tanya don't like the fact that you went off with Cat's boyfriend, and neither do I.'

'What's it to you?'

'You – let yourself down.'

'I'll say! But that's my problem, not yours.'

He thought for a bit. 'No, OK. You're right. Why should I care what you do?'

'What's the latest on Matt by the way?' I asked.

'Gone home with his parents. Can't say I'm sorry.'

'What do you mean?'

'Well. He was a show-off. Tried to impress people. Didn't respect the sea. The Breakneck Rock stunt was crazy, man. The other three were just lucky.' Seth threw up his hands in disgust.

'I heard that they were in for a bit of parental guidance too.'

'Yeah, well. I'd got bored with them. Acting like they were so grown-up.'

'Unlike you lot downstairs! What were you playing?'

Seth sensed that the mood was lifting and his eyes lit up. 'Ooh! Can I go now, miss? I'm not going to explain the game – it would take too long and I have to go home to eat.'

'You can go,' I said, 'as long as you promise to stop giving me a hard time. Matt's not even here now.'

Seth grinned – properly, at last. 'Matt the prat has shot through.' He mimed standing on a surfboard (not hard for Seth) and intoned 'No fear!' at me. Then he set off out of the door and cracked his head on the lintel. I thought we were probably all right again.

Once he'd gone downstairs I couldn't resist a quick list:

Friends
Seth, Harry, Archie, Gideon?
Enemies
Tanya, Cat (though we haven't seen each other), Liza (though
    she hasn't actually said anything).
Neutral
Ivan
and Matt, Luke, Paul and Sebastian have all gone anyway.

Things would be looking up if only I could get things straight with Cat. Seth was right in a way – why did I have to go and spoil everything? Had Matt been worth it? Almost certainly not.

I set up my painting things and started to finalise the figures. I wasn't consciously making the boy look like Gideon, honest. Nor had I realised until now just how much the picture resembled a surfing poster. Oh dear. I'd have to live with that. And though I've been here for years and years I've somehow never managed to see dolphins leaping, so I've had to take them from a photo. Right now they looked as if they were made from rubber. I was going off this picture rapidly.

It was quite a relief to stop for supper, though Dad had to drop me off at the Elliotts again as soon as we'd eaten.

The Elliotts' house is a beautiful old farmhouse with stone flags and nice faded carpets and lots of paintings on the walls. I hadn't quite taken in how lovely it was, first time round. They had a music room, of course, with a harpsichord as well as a grand piano and that's where I was taken. The woodwind players were all adults. Gideon was the only other teenager. He was still shy

105

and inscrutable, but he gave me the old sea-grey gaze as he greeted me. It was strange, being caught in the same small space as one of my 'dolphin boys'.

Nicholas (as I was beginning to think of him) was more relaxed with the smaller group. He called everyone by their Christian names, so I didn't know who they were until I suddenly realised that James, the clarinettist with the Cornish accent, was James Trevarron – my hero! I was so glad I was singing and not playing the clarinet. I've had some singing lessons, but I knew that it was the folky quality of my voice that they were after, so I didn't have to try and do anything different from when I was singing with Seth.

It was all woodwind to start off with. The cellist as the angel came in later. Gideon and I sat and listened while the grown-ups went through the overture. They made a wonderful sound. I couldn't believe I was hearing a private performance by James Trevarron! Then it was Gideon's turn to be the angel arriving like a great rolling, splashing, sparkling wave (Nicholas explained it all before they began). I shut my eyes and listened. Nicholas swished a pair of cymbals along with the cello, and it worked – it did sound like pounding surf. Then the voice of the angel – the solo cello. Then Nicholas played my part on the piano along with the cello, to show how the voices and emotions interwove. I opened my eyes. I'd had a temporary memory lapse about Gideon playing the cello. He was brilliant, even better, maybe, than the amazing violinist on our music course. When he finished, everyone congratulated him, and I picked up from their mutterings about Rostropovitch and the Paris Conservatoire that Gideon was something of a prodigy. 'How old are you, Gideon?' asked James Trevarron.

'He's still fifteen,' said Nicholas proudly. 'OK, Jo? Are you ready to begin?'

'I – I haven't got a highly trained voice,' I reminded him, humbled after hearing Gideon. 'You do know that, don't you?' I didn't want all these professional musicians being disappointed.

'You have a beautiful, *un*tutored voice,' said Nicholas. 'As specified by Max Barnes.' He turned to the musicians. 'She's perfect you know. You're in for a treat.' He did the cymbals with the cello for the wave again and Gideon and I were on our own before the woodwind joined in. I was enjoying myself.

'Excellent!' said Nicholas. 'What do you think, James?'

'Wonderful, my dear,' said James Trevarron. (I couldn't believe it!) 'You've got a lovely clear voice, with just the right amount of throatiness – if you don't mind me saying. Max will be so pleased.'

'OK everybody!' called Nicholas. 'Let's run through it again. Eileen will be appearing with coffee and biscuits in fifteen minutes precisely.'

By the end of the rehearsal the 'Annunication' was up to performance standard. Nicholas said we might run through the piece once tomorrow, but he was more than happy with it. He also didn't want me to be over-rehearsed, or we'd lose the effect he'd been looking for. 'Now, I'm dropping this young reprobate' (Gideon) 'off at the pub – strictly for soft drinks and socialising, I'm told. Is that where you're bound, Jo?'

'Not tonight, no. I've got things to do at home.'

'Oh,' said Gideon. 'I thought you might be going there too.'

'I would,' I said, 'but not tonight, I'm afraid.'

'Of course, I'd forgotten,' said Gideon. 'Those guys – your friends – they've all gone, haven't they?'

'Yes, but that's not why I don't want to go. It's just that – I've got other things to do.' I didn't want to explain about the painting. It sounded so naff. Even though I would really have loved to go down to the pub with Gideon. But the painting had to be finished. So I was taken home and Gideon was driven on to the pub alone.

Ten

On Sunday morning I got up early and finished the picture. I was moderately pleased with it. I'd made the dolphins look less rubbery and the boy/dolphin idea worked quite well. Once Dad put it in the frame it looked more promising. Anyway, it was done.

'You're looking peaky, Josie,' Mum told me at breakfast time.

'I've been busy, Mum. This is worse than term-time – finishing off bits of art and rehearsing till all hours!'

'Then I'm going to take you down to the beach for a blow in the wind. I've hardly seen you this holiday.'

'Do I have to, Mum?'

'Yes. I insist. It's probably going to rain later, so it might be the only time I get down there too. Come along.'

I followed her meekly to the car. As we drove down the hill we had to squeeze past a group of girls – Cat, Tanya and Liza. They were up early. Mum tooted and waved at them in her usual friendly way. They turned away and ignored us.

'What's up with them?' Mum asked. 'They'd usually have jumped at the chance of a lift down to the beach, especially Tanya with that leg.'

'They don't like me any more.'

'What?'

'I did something stupid, and they don't like me any more.'

'Silly girls. What sort of stupid?'

'No, they're not silly, Mum. I deserved it.'

'How could you possibly deserve that sort of rudeness?'

'I'm ashamed to say I, er, got off with Cat's boyfriend when she wasn't there.'

'It takes two to tango,' Mum said drily. 'Do they hate Cat's boyfriend as well?'

'He's not here to hate. He's the one who had the accident. All that crowd of boys has moved on now, and they sort of blame me for that, too, I think.'

We'd arrived at the beach. It was windy and spitting with rain. I wondered if the sun would ever shine in Cornwall again. We walked into the wind, heads bent. 'Have you apologised to Cat?'

'She won't let me.'

'Dear me. It seems to me that you were silly, but

they're not behaving much better. Do you want me to talk to their parents about it?'

I was horrified. 'ABSOLUTELY NO WAY!' I yelled. 'Please, no, Mum. I've got to sort this one out myself. Tomorrow. When all the singing's out of the way.'

'Suit yourself. I just don't want them being mean to you and making you unhappy.'

'It was my fault, Mum. And the guy's.'

'Ooh, I'm glad I'm not a teenager any more.'

The sea always has a calming effect on my brain. I listened to the noise of the waves breaking on the beach. 'Hear that noise, Mum?'

'The waves?'

'They manage to make that sound with a cello and cymbals in the Max Barnes piece. It's really effective.'

'I'm longing to hear it. Dad said that all sorts of famous musicians were playing in it.'

'James Trevarron for one! I'm the only non-professional there. Apart from Gideon Elliott. He plays the cello.'

'I can't believe how you can take it all in your stride.'

'It's not a difficult piece. It's like a Christmas carol or a hymn. And they want me for my "untutored" voice.'

'You wouldn't call it untutored if you'd seen your singing teacher's bills!'

'That was ages ago. And she taught me lots, but I'll never be an opera singer.'

'The main thing is that they chose you and like you.'

'Thanks to Gideon Elliott. He heard me singing with Seth at the barbecue and told his dad. Good job I decided to do the choir thing after all this year! It was only because the girls were being so nasty to me!'

Mum looked at her watch. 'We'd better get you back for your rehearsal. Dad wants to leave a bit early so he can take your picture in.'

'And I want a shower before we go.' I linked my arm in hers and we walked quickly back to the car with the wind behind us.

I spent all day being very aware of Gideon and Caleb but not speaking to them. They were in the row behind me for choir, so they were singing down the back of my neck, and I heard them chatting too. Caleb needles Gideon constantly, but compared to some brothers I know they seem to be good mates. I picked up from someone else that Gideon was two years younger than Caleb, which made Caleb seventeen. They're both fairish with these grey eyes, but Caleb is built more squarely and his hair is crisper and curlier than Gideon's. Gideon is lankier, with longer, straighter hair that flops into his eyes. Shaking his hair off his face is one of Gideon's mannerisms, though when he plays the cello it almost hides his face completely.

They talked a lot about surfing. My ears pricked up when they were discussing some girls they'd met down at the pub, but they didn't mention any names. I was longing to go back down there, but I wasn't quite sure who I'd go with now. Seth maybe. At one point Caleb asked Gideon if he'd seem 'them' yet. That was intriguing, too, but they never said who 'they' were either.

I caught Gideon's eye once or twice during the day. He was looking at me, I know, but we never said anything. We had a run-through of the 'Annunciation' after lunch when the players had arrived for the afternoon rehearsal, and the two of us complimented one another, but I couldn't think what else to say to him. It was frustrating, because I was beginning to feel we might have quite a lot to say if only we knew where to begin.

Everyone in the choir was dressed for the concert in a holiday version of white tops and black bottoms. I had on a short white top and some baggy black trousers. The younger men and boys were in white T-shirts and black shorts. We were doing scales and warming up exercises in the church hall where the art exhibition was still being mounted. I couldn't see my picture in the children's section anywhere. Then I spotted it on the wall in the main exhibition. I panicked at first because I felt it looked so amateurish in comparison with some of the paintings there, but then I had a moment of pride. It wasn't so bad! The light caught the glitter of the splashes very satisfactorily – it was going to be quite an evening for surf, what with the 'Annunication' and everything!

We filed into the little church. The rain had stopped and the sky was clearing. It was still light outside, but there were candles waiting to be lit for the second half of the concert once the sun went down. We were starting with the Haydn and finishing with the Handel, with the three songs in between – two at the end of the first half and the 'Annunciation' before the Handel. I was excited rather than nervous – a healthy adrenalin rush pumped through me. The first half was lovely – Nicholas just brought the best out of everybody in the Haydn. Then the first two songs, which were also sea songs, one by

Benjamin Britten and one by Vaughan Williams, both sung by professionals. I had a moment of sheer terror when I thought of myself standing up there, but then I remembered that I was merely another 'player' in the Barnes. I wouldn't be so exposed.

I felt a bit jittery in the interval. The crush in the church hall was incredible. Mum and Tim were there to support Dad and me, though neither of them are particularly musical. Tim came back with his hands full of plastic cups of orange squash and wine, and a couple of wrapped Kitkats held between his teeth. When he'd unburdened himself he told us that he'd heard loads of people commenting on my picture. 'I reckon quite a lot of people are going to put in bids for it. I saw Cat's parents looking at it and they sounded quite keen to buy it.'

'Cat's not here, is she?' I don't think I could have coped with that.

'No, but Tanya's been dragged along to hear Ivan.'

'Don't you let those horrid girls put you off your singing, dear,' said Mum.

'It's only Tanya,' I said. 'I'm amazed they persuaded her to come to anything as dorky as a concert in a church.' I peered in the direction of my painting. 'And can you all keep quiet about my picture? I don't want people to know I did it just yet, especially as it's not in the children's section.'

'You never know,' said Dad. 'You might make some money!'

Nicholas Elliott was beckoning me. 'Wish me luck,' I said and made my way over to him, along with Gideon and the other musicians.

Gideon was chattering nervously. 'I don't know about you, but I'll be happier when this is over.'

'I'm not too bad,' I said. 'Anyway, you don't strike me as someone who gets nervous.'

'I suppose I'm fine once I get going. It's just this bit I don't like. The waiting.' It was a conversation, of a sort. I liked his resonant voice. I even quite liked the hair-tossing mannerism. It gave the gaze a better chance. We went into the church and set up our chairs and stands. The players tuned up. I didn't need to warm up – I'd been singing all day. We got into our positions. Unlike the other players I was standing, but not out at the front. Gideon and I were at the top of the semicircle facing Nicholas. Nicholas gave us a little pep talk before the audience came back in. 'You two,' he said to me and Gideon, 'is there any chance that you can look at one another in your duet? It is a dialogue. Give it a little try.' My part was simple – I didn't need the music, but Gideon knew his as well. We tried the first few lines. Nicholas was right – it gave the notes a kind of buzz.

'I can do it,' said Gideon, 'if you can.'

'It's not a problem for me,' I said. 'I've got the words fixed in my brain.'

'Think you can both do it?' said Nicholas.

'Yes,' we chorused, and the audience started coming back in and taking their seats. The candles had been lit. 'Typical Dad,' said Gideon to me as we waited to start. 'It's one of his trademarks. Get performers to do something just a little bit different at the last minute. He always says it "makes the music more exciting and immediate." '

'Help.'

'No, it works. Don't worry Jo – I'll look after you!' That's what he said. It was so lovely. He shook back his hair and smiled at me.

Nichlas gave a little spiel before we began about the *Madonna of the Waves* etc, and the fact that the piece had its roots in folk music. And we were off. Something about the candlelit church made the music quite magical. The woodwind sounded watery and the cymbal clash with the cello was perfect. I turned to face Gideon during the Angel words (which meant I didn't have to look at the audience) and then we managed to look at one another as he played and I sang. It was like a dance or a conversation – very intimate, as if we were communicating at an immensely profound level. I could see Gideon, and I was conscious of Nicholas's baton, but I wasn't aware of anyone else beyond the barrier of candlelight. It was over almost too quickly. Nicholas hushed the audience's applause to make a further announcement. He wanted to thank the performers but he particularly wanted to thank Max Barnes for writing the piece and, wait for it, would Max himself like to come and take a bow . . .

A marvellous white-haired whiskery gentleman came up to the front. I was so glad I hadn't known beforehand that the composer was going to be listening. 'Did you know about this?' I mouthed at Gideon, and he nodded. They must have realised it would freak me out to tell me.

Max Barnes came and gave us each a hug. 'The future of music is obviously in safe hands,' he said. Then he made his way back into the audience and Gideon and I rejoined the choir for the Handel.

It was so strange when the concert was finished. All that

work – and it was over. And the 'Annunication' – my moment of glory – had passed! More to the point, for me, my time with Gideon had ended almost before it had begun. So weird to have experienced something so intense with him. I felt he was mine!

Mum and Dad took me home. Tim informed me that Ivan and Tanya were going down for a last half hour or so at the pub with Caleb and Gideon, but I was suddenly exhausted. I certainly didn't want to cope with Cat and co. 'You were impressive, big sister,' said Tim. 'Pity I couldn't see you.'

'Yes, that was a shame,' said Mum. 'That's the only problem with a concert in a church. It's hard to see over people's heads.'

'So you couldn't see that Gideon and I were meant to look as if we were having a conversation?'

'I could,' Dad said. 'It lifted the whole performance another few notches – if that was possible! The bigwig musos were thrilled. You're a clever little girl, Josie Liddell!'

'With such a modest dad,' said Mum. I let her make me some cocoa when we got in.

'When will I know how much I get for my painting?' I asked Dad.

'Ah, now. I did ask. The bidding goes on until Wednesday, but I was able to discover that you have five bids already, and the highest is £80!'

'Wow! Really?' I couldn't believe it. 'Any chance of a loan of £40 against that? I'm broke. Don't ask me why.'

'I expect so,' said Mum. 'Go on, go to bed, you look finished.'

*

I had loads of lists to write:

Highs this holiday

1 Doing the Annunciation with Gideon.
2 Getting off with Matt (despite the train tracks).
3 Hearing that I might have made £80 with my crappy old painting!

Lows this holiday

1 Spending all my money on one round of drinks.
2 Tanya and Liza being horrible to me.
3 Cat not speaking to me.
4 Hearing that Matt had had an accident.
5 Falling out with Seth.
6 Having to wear a brace this year of all years.

Hmm. The lows were still winning, but the highs were all good highs.

Things I like(d) about Matt

1 Goodlooking
2 Sexy
3 Sure I'll think of some more . . .

Things I like about Gideon

1 Eyes
2 Hair
3 Shyness
4 Voice
5 Body – surfer's body and quite tall.
6 Fantastic musician
7 Being 'Gideon's Virgin' and him thinking I can sing.

8 The way he called me Jo and said he'd look after me.
9 Doesn't appear to have a girlfriend.

Hmm. Gideon's good points far outweighed Matt's. But though I really liked him, and felt that I already had a sort of relationship with him, I couldn't imagine getting off with him. Especially as I had a very clear memory of getting off with Matt. What a mess.

I went to sleep more determined than ever to make my peace with Cat. Apart from anything else, I was going to need some friends to do things with now the singing was over.

Eleven

There's nothing quite like the bliss of waking up in a seaside cottage with the sun forcing its way through the gaps in the curtains and the gulls calling outside. I must have slept for hours.

I lay there for a while feeling cosy. Great! No pressure. Painting completed. Performance over. Both satisfactory.

I thought about Matt and me in the dunes for a bit, but the memory had become like a film where the part of Josie was played by someone else. Then I thought about Gideon and me in the 'Annunication'. That was definitely me. I had been through all those emotions –

of fear, of awe and of love – in the space of six minutes. I say 'love'. I hadn't fallen in love with Gideon, or not in the way I was used to. It wasn't like chatting someone up and hoping they'd snog you at the end of the evening. But we'd definitely shared a pretty intense emotional experience.

I felt a new set of lists coming on but, all of a sudden, breakfast seemed a more appealing option. I wrapped my dressing-gown around me, leading-lady style, and swanned down the stairs.

Tim was dressed and ready to go. 'Surf's up!' he said. 'It's going to be a perfect day. Your mates would be kicking themselves if they could see what they're missing. You coming, Jose?'

'You must be kidding. Boogie boarding in gentle waves is all I can cope with. Your sort of surfing's far too scary.'

I helped myself to breakfast. Mum and my aunt were packing a picnic. Dad, my uncle and the kids had gone somewhere else. 'Hi, love!' called Mum. 'I've just been telling Pat about your concert last night.'

'You don't half hide your light under a bushel,' said Pat. 'No one in my family can sing to save their lives. I suppose Alan's got a good voice. I used to be impressed when he belted out the hymns at our friends' weddings.'

'Just like Jim, probably,' said Mum. 'And Josie's inherited it. She certainly doesn't get it from me.'

'Did you have to audition?' said Pat. 'I wouldn't fancy an audition.'

'No,' I said. 'I wouldn't have liked that either. I didn't do anything – one of the conductor's sons heard me singing with Seth on the beach.'

'Talk of the devil,' said my mum. 'Seth's on his way down to the beach right now.' I peered round her, out of the kitchen window. Seth was gliding past on his skateboard, surfboard over his shoulder, followed by Cat on her bike, also carrying a surfboard. Damn. I'd been hoping to talk to Cat today. I had this feeling that if I got her on her own, I could make her realise that I was genuinely sorry. We go back such a long way, I really didn't want us to end up hating each other.

Tim was pacing up and down. 'Wish Dad would get back,' he said. 'He promised me a lift. I'm going to miss the good waves if I don't get there soon.'

'Shall I take him?' Pat asked Mum.

'Would you?' said Mum. 'It would take the pressure off the others. I'll let them know that's what's happening.' She started dialling Dad's mobile number.

'What about you, Josie?' asked my aunt.

'No, I'm going to slob around here for a bit longer, thanks.' Pat whisked Tim away.

Mum put the phone down. 'Hey, guess what? Dad called in at the church hall to see how the bids on your painting were going. He said the £80 bid came from one of the Elliotts!'

'Wow. The Elliotts? Cool! No one's supposed to know that. Whose arm did Dad twist? Can they just stop the bidding and let the Elliotts have it? I'd be ecstatically happy with £72 or whatever.'

'No. They always close it on the Wednesday evening at the do. Don't you remember? Glass of plonk to make people up their bids still further (in case someone else has offered more) and then at a certain time they draw a

line under the offers and stick the successful buyers'
names on the paintings. I helped one year.'

'Do I get to go to the do?'

'Of course, if you want to. You always went when you
were little.'

'But I just whizzed around outside, and you always
bought my paintings.'

'Exactly. This will be much more exciting.'

'How long till you go down to the beach?'

'Dad won't be back now for an hour or so.'

'Great. I'm going to have a long bath.'

I was fretting about Cat. It was more than four days since
we'd last spoken. We'd had tiffs before, but none had
ever lasted this long. Cat's fun, Cat's my mate. She's a bit
difficult at times, and she always has to be ahead of the
game, but I've always known that. I so don't want us not
to be friends. It's always been Josie and Cat, in Cornwall.
Tanya and Liza are around, but it's always been me and
my family that Cat has spent time with while her
parents went in search of culture (as Dad said – so why
come to Cornwall and not Venice?).

I couldn't quite believe what had come over me last
week. I'd really wanted to impress Matt, that's for sure.
I'd had this barmy idea that being in with Matt somehow meant being in with all the others. If only I could
have plumped for Luke. And where was the beautiful
Bathsheba now? I suppose it's quite likely that there's
another whole group of people arrived this weekend.
That was a cheering thought. Perhaps there would be
new boys for all of us! I washed my hair and shaved my
legs extra carefully.

I've got several bikinis. I tried on one I haven't worn so far, a silvery one, and regarded myself in the mirror. I looked OK. On the skinny side, especially my legs, but not embarrassingly so. My hair's a bit wispy, and the brace is horrendous – but from a distance I look fairly normal. My skin's going pink – it will go slightly brown eventually. I peered at my face in the mirror. And I've got some spots. Great. I whacked on some make-up to hide them, and put on a pair of shorts and a top. And then changed them for a sarong and a top. And then changed the top for a chiffon blouse and tied the ends together to show off my midriff. Then I got involved in drawing a pretend tattoo with a biro just above my right hip bone. Then Mum called me and it was time to go down to the beach.

'You look very swish,' said Uncle Alan.

'He means "nice",' said my dad, laughing. 'And don't make her self-conscious, Alan. It's hell being a teenage girl, isn't it Josie?'

'Huh. Yes,' I said, thinking about the mess I was in with Cat and co.

As soon as we got down to the beach I could see exactly where my family were going to position themselves. Practically next to the rocks where Tanya, her plaster-cast leg sticking out, and Liza were sitting. My one-time friends ignored me, so I ignored them. I laid out my towel, stripped down to my bikini, slapped on some suntan lotion, put on my sunglasses and settled down to read. The one thing I'd forgotten was my Discman. So I couldn't completely block out what Tanya was saying to Liza.

'. . . dragged along to this *awful* concert in a church, just because my dorky brother and all these other tragic people were singing classical music . . .'

Oh well, I suppose I might have complained in the same way myself if I hadn't been part of it.

'. . . a bit *amateur*. I mean, if someone's singing a solo you do expect them to have a really strong voice . . .'

I began to realise Tanya was intent on winding me up. The only thing was to get out of earshot. I tied on my sarong and drifted down to the sea. The breeze whipped the soft material about my legs and swept my hair off my face. I felt a solitary soul as I stepped through the shallows. I walked almost as far as I could and then had to turn round and come back. My little cousins were running towards me to tell me that they were starting the picnic, so I had to return.

'. . . tattoos are incredibly affected, don't you?'

'I wonder when she got that done?' That was Liza speaking – and it wasn't meant for my ears! They really thought I had a tattoo! And I knew they were dead jealous, because we'd been talking about it last week. Cat was thinking up something new to shock her parents with.

I helped myself to some sandwiches and crisps, which were noisy to eat, so I didn't hear what they were saying for a while, whether or not I was intended to. Then I offered to build sandcastles with my cousins further down the beach, which they were thrilled about. 'I can't imagine why anyone would want to plaster themselves with make-up to come to the beach,' was the only other Tanya comment I heard – she must have gauged the exact speed and direction of the wind.

We built a brilliant sandcastle with moats and flags. And then I moulded a car out of the sand for them to sit in. And all the time I managed to stay just far enough away from Tanya and Liza, though it hadn't escaped my notice that Liza wasn't the one dishing out the dirt. It was funny though, because Tanya isn't really that catty. It was almost as if it she was playing a game. But if the desired result was to make me feel unhappy, then they'd definitely succeeded.

'How about a swim, Josie?' Mum had got up and was walking around in a hideous swimsuit. I wanted to protect her from the critical gaze of the two girls, but I felt pretty embarrassed to be seen with her myself.

'OK, Mum, but please put a towel round you!'

As we went down to the water, Mum said, 'I hope it's not Liza and Tanya's opinion that you're worried about. Because I tell you, if they carry on making bitchy comments just within earshot I am going to go over and – and – I don't know, kick sand in their faces or something!'

'I didn't realise you could hear them.'

'Well, I can, and I don't like it.'

'If I could only make it up with Cat, it would be a lot better, but I just can't catch her. She's avoiding me.'

'You could do a note, perhaps?'

'Good idea, Mum. Maybe I'll do that tonight if I don't manage to speak to her.'

Tim needed fetching and it was time to go back up to the cottage. Tim was full of his day's surfing. 'It was wicked today! Caleb and Gideon were with us. And Seth. And Cat. She's pretty good – for a girl!'

'Do you mean to say she spoke to you?'

'Not as such. I was with Seth, anyway. She was more interested in the other two.'

'But did she blank you?'

'Not really. Dad gave Seth and her a lift home, too.'

I couldn't believe it. 'Dad? Did you really give Cat a lift? You know she's not speaking to me?'

'Oh, isn't she?' Dad said vaguely. 'Well, she's speaking to me.'

'That's because you didn't get off with her boyfriend, Dad!' said Tim.

'Enough!' I said, and glared at Tim. I felt wretched. Tanya and Liza were one thing, but Cat being chummy with all my friends and family but not me was another.

'Has Dad told you about this evening?' Tim asked me, changing the subject.

'No. What about this evening?'

Dad filled me in. 'Half-price water-ski lessons. I booked you and Tim in. I know you've always wanted to try it, and two for the price of one seemed like a good deal.'

That cheered me up a bit. 'Excellent. What time are we going?'

'After supper. Half-past seven. Is that OK?'

'You bet!' I went up to my room. The thought of Cat being friendly with Gideon and Caleb didn't exactly thrill me either. Or the fact that she could surf with the boys. It meant that she could be with them when I couldn't. Even Seth. And as for new boys – I couldn't go down to the pub on my own, so I wasn't going to meet any, was I? And it all came back to the same thing. I'd got off with Matt, my best friend's boyfriend. What an idiot.

Tim and I waited down by the water for our lesson. It was a stunning evening. The wind had dropped and we were quite sheltered. Dad had taken off over the dunes with the labrador. It's weird because I've been past the water-ski-ing school so many times but never come down below the road here. It's spitting distance from the pub but you can't see one from the other.

Tim went water-ski-ing first and came back in a high old state of excitement. 'We saw dolphins!' he said. 'Only one or two. Unfortunately we scared them away, but that's the first time I've seen them!'

I asked the instructor to take me out to the same place, which he did, but either I was concentrating so hard on holding on and staying upright, or the dolphins had disappeared, because I never saw them. The water ski-ing was great though. Whizzing over the water like a surfer, but without having to do all the work yourself!

Dad and Taffy (the labrador) were sitting on the wall with Tim when I got back. 'Thanks, Dad, that was brilliant.'

'Did you see the dolphins, too?' Tim asked. 'Dad did.'

'No. You'd frightened them all away.'

'Shame,' said Dad. 'They were a splendid sight.'

'Crazy, isn't it?' I said. 'I've sold a painting of them for loads of money, but I've still never actually seen one.'

We were walking towards the car. 'You will,' said Dad, 'when things are going a bit better for you. Your grandfather had some little rhyme about "see dolphins play when the world goes your way". Dolphins are kind of magic. We all know that.'

'Things are certainly going my way,' said Tim to me in the car. 'I met this girl today, called Cleopatra! She's got a sister called Bathsheba. And she thinks I'm great.'

'How do you know?' I asked him.

'Because she said so!'

Of course I'd forgotten that we'd have to inch our way through the crowd outside the pub. Luckily I was in the back seat, so I couldn't really be seen. I could *see*, though. And what I saw was this: three boys and three girls – Seth, Caleb and Gideon with Cat, Tanya and Liza. Cat was doing an impression of someone surfing – she must have been telling them about something that had happened today. And they were obviously all having a brilliant time, Seth included. No wonder I hadn't spotted any dolphins.

Dear Cat,
I know you'll never forgive me for kissing Matt when you weren't there,

(I thought I'd stick to this story until I had to say more)

But I'm really VERY, VERY SORRY, and I didn't set out to do it – it just happened.

(Actually that wasn't strictly true, but I hadn't expected Cat not to turn up. I never dreamed it would actually happen.)

I know you must hate me, but please talk to me and let me apologise properly. I really want us to be friends again.

Love from Josie   XXXXXX

I stuck some shiny stickers on the envelope, went up the lane and posted it through her door.

Twelve

By midday I'd given up hope of Cat rushing round in response to my note and went shopping in one of the nearby towns with my parents. They advanced me some of my painting money, so I was able to buy a few bits of make-up and some presents for my friends, though I'd have to wait to get Holly's. We bought pasties for lunch and took them home.

After yesterday's winds it was still and grey, and the sea was flat. Tim was mooching round disconsolately. He wanted an excuse to be in the same place as the girl he'd met, Cleo, and surfing was the only one he could think of, but today just wasn't a day for it. I decided to call on Seth, since he'd probably be in the same mood as Tim, and in need of company.

I went up to his cottage after lunch. He was there, taking refuge from his family by reading in his room. His mum pointed me up the stairs. 'Seth?' I called.

'Hi!' He didn't look too fed up that it was me.

'I know it's flat today – thought you might like some company.'

'Where've you been, Josie? I haven't seen you around.'

'You know where I've been. Singing all Sunday. And then yesterday you were off surfing, so you wouldn't have seen me anyway.'

'Thought you might have come down to the pub.'

'No one to go with, have I?'

'Oh, I think the girls have simmered down.'

'Tanya hasn't. She was near us on the beach yesterday, making bitchy comments just within earshot. Even my mum heard them.'

'Well, you know Tanya. Anyway, she's missing that guy – the first ever guy to kiss her, according to Cat – how's that? So she's kind of taking it out on everyone.'

'She looked OK at the pub last night,' I said.

'How do you know that?' Seth was puzzled.

'We drove past after a water-ski lesson. I saw you all.'

'Oh, poor little Miss Nobody-loves-me! Come on, Josie,' said Seth, rubbing my wrist sympathetically. 'Listen – come down to the pub with me tonight. You can have a ride on my skateboard. I think it's time you all made friends. Especially now those cretinous guys have gone away. You can see how desperate the girls are, they're even talking to me!'

'Thanks, Seth. It's Cat I care about. We've always been friends. Like you and me have always been friends.'

'We-ll,' said Seth. 'You do have to treat friends like friends . . . Anyway. Let's play some music. I gather our little gig on the beach got you some more work. Wish I'd heard it now. Even Caleb said it was good.'

'Tanya thought it was rubbish.'

'Pah! What does Tanya know? Stop talking! Sing!'

Gideon and Caleb were not at the pub. Cat, Tanya and Liza were. 'Come on, girls,' said Seth. 'Make up!'

'I'll buy everyone a drink,' I said, 'because I want to say I'm sorry. I've made some money, so I can afford it.'

'Ooh, what on?' said Cat, intrigued. But none of this lot knew my painting was in an exhibition. I thought I'd better wait until I knew it had been sold.

'Sold her body, probably,' said Tanya, refusing to be mollified.

'Not quite,' I said. 'But I have sold something. I'll tell you on Thursday.'

'Cokes all round, then,' said Seth. 'Give me your money, Josie. I'll get them.'

'Did you get my note?' I asked Cat, anxiously.

'Yup,' said Cat, and then, quickly, 'Liza said you've got a tattoo. When did you do that?'

'Shall I show you my tattoo?' I said.

'Go on, then,' said Cat. Liza turned away from her conversation with Tanya to have a look, as I pulled the waistband of my jeans down over my hip. The biro had faded somewhat.

'Hey! It's a fake!' said Tanya.

'Of course it is,' I said.

'I thought you might have gone to Newquay with your little brother,' said Tanya.

'It's quite realistic,' said Liza. 'Would you do one for me?'

'And me,' said Cat.

'What are you all looking at?' said Seth, coming back with five Cokes.

'Josie's tattoo,' said Liza.

'I didn't know you had a tattoo?' said Seth. 'Let's see.' I rolled down my waistband again. He peered at it. 'It's not real, is it? Good dolphins though.'

'Uhuh,' I said non-committally. I wondered where Gideon and Caleb were, but I didn't want to be the one that asked.

Cat was tapping her fingers and looking bored. She'd spoken to me. That was good, but I can't say I felt forgiven. I sipped my drink. Liza talked about Sebastian. She and Tanya were hatching a plan to visit the boys further down the coast before they left Cornwall altogether. I was itching to know how Matt was, but that was a name I certainly had no intention of introducing.

'How's Matt, Cat?' said Seth.

'How should I know?' said Cat, her eyes raking the pub crowd for someone or other.

'What's on for tomorrow, then?' said Seth.

No one answered.

'Anyone fancy the bike ride?' I ventured.

'OK,' said Cat, surprisingly. 'If there's no surf.'

'I don't know why you're so keen on surfing all of a sudden,' said Tanya crabbily. 'You know I can't do any of these things with my leg.'

'It's those boys, isn't it, Cat?' said Liza. 'I fancy the bike ride, though. Can't not do any of the usual things, Tanya, just because of you.'

'We're doing something anyway,' said Tanya. 'Some garden in a clay pit. Ivan's been going on about it.'

'Ellie's boys went there. It's amazing, apparently.'

'Bike ride, Seth?'

'Not really. I expect I'll go over and see what the waves are like anyway.'

Seth seemed disappointed about something. 'Tim will come with you,' I said.

'I'm going to get another drink,' said Cat. 'But you lot will have to give me the money if you want one.'

'Have your parents still stopped your allowance then, Cat?' asked Liza.

'Yes. Ironic, isn't it?' said Cat as we all counted out coins for her.

'They stopped it after they caught her with Matt,' said Tanya pointedly to me.

'As Cat said,' I replied, 'it's ironic.' We followed her with our eyes. She stopped to chat to a group of lads on the way in to the pub.

'Who are they?' asked Liza.

'Some surfers we met yesterday,' said Seth, waving at them.

'Hope Cat brings them over,' said Liza.

'She's hardly likely to, with *her* here, is she?' said Tanya.

'Excuse me,' said Seth, 'I'm just going to go and have a word with them.'

'Daft hippie,' said Tanya, as soon as he'd left us.

'Seth's OK!' I said.

'Oh! Standing up for our friends are we now?' said Tanya.

'Shut up, Tanya,' said Liza. 'I'm fed up with you going on and on.' Tanya slumped back in a sulk. 'She's missing Paul, aren't you, Tanya? And her cast's getting her down, isn't it, Tanya? I miss Sebastian, but it doesn't mean I'm not interested in new talent. That guy Seth's talking to looks pretty yummy.' Cat arrived. 'Are you keeping those lads to yourself, Cat?' said Liza.

'Oh, I was only asking them something,' said Cat. 'Drink up, everyone. My dad will be here to take me away any minute now. And anyone else who wants a lift.'

When the others went, I joined Seth and the new boys. They were OK in a surfing sort of way. They all talked surf-speak. I'd thought Matt and the others were cool when they talked like that, but I wasn't so impressed this time. Seth and I walked home together, about a mile and a half in the dark (could have been romantic with someone else). It was restful, though, to be with a friend. 'Did you meet those guys with Cat?' I asked him.

'Yeah,' he said. 'And Caleb and Gideon. That's who Cat was asking after. They weren't here tonight.'

'Does she know I know them?'

'I doubt it. Don't muscle in on those two, Josie, please. I wouldn't be able to rescue you a second time.'

'I wouldn't dare,' I said, reeling. (Gideon was *mine*!) 'Thanks for tonight, Seth. It's great that Cat's talking to me again. And the bike ride will be good. Sure you don't want to come?'

'Look at me, Josie. In case you'd forgotten, I'm not built for cycling.' I stopped and looked at him. He stopped too, and then flinched. His brace shone in his querulous half smile, just like mine must have been. 'On the other hand, don't look at me like that. I'm not sure I can cope.' And he loped on ahead, leaving me to scamper along after him.

Mum drove us to the bike hire place. Liza nudged me. 'Hey, it's the guy we all fancied last year!'

'Hello, girls. What can I do for you?' He was gorgeous.

I dug Cat in the ribs while Liza stammered her request for a mountain bike, but she didn't really respond. 'That one please,' Cat said when it was her turn. Not a flicker of a giggle or a blush. It took me several minutes to choose mine. We set off on the trail, a cycle path that follows an old railway track to the fishing port where I'd seen Holly's present.

Cat cycled on ahead. 'I might even dump Sebastian if *that* guy asked me out,' said Liza as we rode side by side behind Cat.

'Cat didn't seem very interested.'

'That's because she's interested in someone else.'

'You mean Matt?'

'No. Well, he's not around, is he?'

'Who then?'

'Dunno. She won't say. Someone she met surfing the other day I think. I don't think she'd be talking to you now if Matt was the only guy in her life!'

'I suppose not.'

We struggled uphill, and neither of us spoke for a while. Cat was some way in front. 'Liza?'

'What?'

'I know I did a terrible thing, but it was Matt as well, you know.'

'Hardly the point, Josie. Imagine how you'd feel if someone did that to you – especially a friend.'

That was the trouble. I couldn't really imagine it. People at school have treated me badly in all sorts of ways – I'm used to it, but no one's ever nicked a boyfriend. I've never really had a real boyfriend anyway. It's either been admiring from afar or a quick grope at a party. I was upset when the drummer on the music course started going out with someone else, but that just seemed inevitable at the time. No, I couldn't imagine how Cat felt.

Cat had stopped and was sitting on the bank at the side of the track swigging from a bottle of water. 'You guys are so unfit!' she laughed. 'You wouldn't last five minutes surfing!'

'Don't expect I would,' I said meekly, getting off my bike.

'Neither would you if you'd spent the week chaperoning Tanya,' said Liza. She threw her bike down. 'Ooh, my bum is sore already!'

'This bike's more comfortable than my own,' said Cat. 'I don't mind being with Tanya if I'm not surfing, Liza. You can do things with Josie.'

I don't know how Liza felt, but I found that statement quite hurtful. I busied myself with my rucksack and found a drink and packet of biscuits. 'Biscuit, anyone?' Liza took one. Cat declined. Cat usually eats more than anyone.

We set off again. It's a great ride, sore backsides apart, with loads of people on the trail on tandems, tricycles, little trailers with babies in. It would be impossible to spend the whole time worrying, and as time went by Cat was whooping and cheering with us as we went over bumps and dips, over the old railway bridge, skirted the sea and finally arrived at the fishing port and padlocked our bikes together.

We bought ourselves chips and sat by the harbour watching the world go by.

'Hey-eh!' said Liza. 'Look over there!' It was Luke and Paul. No Matt, obviously, but no Sebastian either. The two of them looked unremarkable on their own amongst the other tourists – just a couple of teenage boys, one of them fairly unprepossessing. I didn't want to talk to them. Memories of their wretched competition and where it had landed me made me want to forget them altogether. But Liza ran over to greet them while Cat and I sat and watched from a distance.

'Don't you want to go and say hello?' I asked her.

'Nah,' she said, and turned to face the sea.

'No, neither do I. I hope Liza doesn't bring them over.'

Liza didn't bring them over. While she was with them Bathsheba came and claimed Luke and a strange girl (who looked like the back of a bus, Liza said) linked arms with Paul, so it was embarrassment all round. Sebastian had already gone home, but Liza knew that – they were still in contact.

'We don't tell Tanya, OK?' said Liza when she came back to report and Cat and I nodded in agreement. 'Gosh! Last week seems so long ago,' she said wistfully. And then realised that last week wasn't a tactful subject for discussion with Cat and me, so she leapt to her feet and dragged us off to the shops. I'd seen some of those beads you thread your hair through for Holly – they had tiny shells on them and I thought they'd look lovely in her dark hair, like a mermaid. I have to admit I bought some for myself too. We bought fudge as well before setting off on the return journey.

There were fewer people on the trail going back. Liza started singing a song that was in the charts and Cat and I joined in. It was almost like old times. Almost.

Dad was picking us up at five so that I could be ready in time for the art do. I didn't particularly want to talk about it to Cat or Liza, but I couldn't stop Dad blathering on as we drove home.

'Oh, that,' said Cat. 'I think my parents are going. They said they'd already put a bid in for something I'd like. I suppose your picture's in the kiddie section, is it, Josie?'

Fortunately, Dad was concentrating on the traffic at that moment, so I just mumbled something in reply. I really wasn't going to say, 'no, it's in the adult section actually' to Cat in her current unpredictable mood.

'How was your cycle ride?' Mum asked when I came in. 'Are the other girls being nicer to you now, darling?'

'It was good,' I said. Sometimes Mum's over-protectiveness really gets to me. Sometimes I think it's why I get picked on in the first place. I went straight up to have a shower and change. I put on some clean jeans and my new top. I looked closely at my face. The spots had gone and my skin had a bit of colour in it. I decided to wear a bit of eyeliner and nothing more. Quite radical for me!

'Hurry up Jo-jo,' Dad was calling. 'The suspense is killing me. I can't wait to find out who's bought your painting and how much they've paid for it!' Tim was out with my uncle and aunt and cousins, so it was just me and my parents heading for the church hall.

The art auction was quite a feature of some people's holidays. It was advertised in all the local papers and, because one or two well known Cornish artists submitted paintings anonymously along with complete novices, it was possible to pick up a bargain. The church hall was buzzing. I felt nervous – more nervous in some ways than when I had been about to perform the Barnes. The drinks were on long trestle tables covered in white cloths at one end of the hall. The business part went on at the other end. Each picture had a number sticker. When the bidding was closed, the names of the final buyers were called out. Buyers didn't discover the artist until they paid up.

I stood with Mum while Dad fetched us drinks. I recognised quite a few faces from the concert. I spotted Gideon looking at my painting and my heart missed a beat. The only time I'd seen him since the concert was when we'd driven past the pub and he'd been with my friends. I remembered seeing him and Caleb for the first time – my dolphin boys, gazing out to sea. They'd seemed mysterious then – they still were in some ways. And somewhere along the line I'd had this 'relationship' with Gideon, this exchange. *He was mine.* That was the phrase that always popped into my head. I watched him from a distance. He stood in front of the painting for some time before going back to Caleb and pointing it out to him. Of course – the Elliotts were paying £80 for it! Weird (but wonderful) to think of my dolphins on a wall of their house with all the other paintings. Flattering!

I saw Cat's parents, and Tanya's too. I followed Gideon round the room with my eyes. He looked good today in a faded blue teeshirt and pale shorts. I noticed his legs for the first time – surfer's legs (now they are nice)! I wanted to go and talk to him, but I felt terribly shy. I didn't know where I'd begin.

But then he must have felt me looking at him, because he suddenly glanced up and caught my eye. He smiled at me with his eyes – I could tell, even across that space, and started to walk towards me. 'Hi Jo,' he said. 'What are you doing here?'

'Oh, just looking,' I said.

'My little brother's got a painting in the children's section. My mum and dad will buy it.'

'That's what my parents used to do with my pictures. I didn't know you had a *little* brother.'

'Oh yes – Ebbie. Ebenezer. Another good old Cornish name, I'm afraid. But since he's going to be a conductor when he grows up he won't mind.'

'Where is he?'

'Over there.' He pointed. And there was a miniature Gideon, floppy hair and all, about six years old. 'Mistake, according to Dad, but we don't tell him that. He's a gas. Ebbie!' he called. 'Ebz – come over here and meet my friend Jo.'

Ebbie came over. 'I know her,' he said. 'She's your Virgin, isn't she? I saw her singing with you.'

Gideon was embarrassed. 'Not funny any more, Ebz,' he said. 'Ignore him, Jo,' he added, and then switched into distant gaze mode. 'Oh, there's my new friend! See you in a bit—' and dashed off. I tried to see who this new friend was, but Ebbie was pulling on my arm to get my attention. 'See that picture over there?' he said. 'My mum and dad are buying it for my brother. At least, they want to.'

'Which picture?' I asked him.

'That one,' he said. Dad had been right. Ebbie was pointing at my picture.

Ebbie drifted off and I went back to my parents. Then I saw who Gideon's new friend was. It was Cat.

Someone banged a gavel. 'Ladies and gentlemen, you have five minutes to make your final bids. There are twelve people here waiting to add them to their lists. Ladies and gentlemen, the bidding will cease in five minutes and we will announce the buyers' names after that.'

I looked over at my painting. Cat was standing in front of it with her parents. Gideon was conferring with them and then Cat and Gideon shot over to his parents, who then rushed over to the desk. 'Well,' said Cat's mum, seeing us as she walked away, 'I just hope no one else is in the running for that picture. I wanted it for Cat but she wants her new boyfriend to have it, so they might just have to up their bid. I've already offered £150.'

Dad winked at me. 'We are talking about the dolphin painting, aren't we?'

'Oh yes,' said Cat's mum.

'Perhaps you ought to warn them then,' said my dad, wickedly, 'that I've just bid £200.'

'Oh gracious!' said Cat's mum, and ran after Cat and Gideon.

'Tee hee,' said dad. 'That's put the cat amongst the pigeons!'

'Dad!'

Cat's new boyfriend? Please, not Gideon. Please don't let Cat want my picture for *my* Gideon.

*

I went outside. I sat on the raised tombstone and looked at the sea, the dusky grey sea. Gideon. Gideon. My Gideon. My dolphin boy. And I was Gideon's Virgin. Please God, not Cat and Gideon, I couldn't bear it. I felt tears rising. She didn't even know. She didn't even know I knew him, let alone – loved – him.

Was that it? Was I in love with him? Surely it didn't have anything to do with the fact that he was 'Cat's boyfriend'? I'd loved him all along, hadn't I?

'Couldn't you stand the suspense?' Dad sat down next to me. 'Come on, they've nearly reached yours.' We went back in.

'. . . and picture number 166 goes to Nicholas Elliott for – £250!'

I didn't speak to Gideon after that. I'd receive a cheque in the post and Cat and Gideon would get a shock to discover the artist, but it wouldn't hurt them half as much as the sight of her skipping over to him and throwing her arms round him hurt me.

Thirteen

'Pub?' said Seth, poking his head round the front door. I was sitting listlessly turning the pages of a magazine.

'No thanks.' I said. 'But thanks for asking.'

'Oh, go on! Cat's in a very good mood this evening. I

hear the bike ride was a success. She went to the art thing, too, didn't she?'

'Yes.'

'She's already down at the pub with Gideon and his brother. They're celebrating, apparently. You never know, someone might buy you a drink!'

'No thanks.'

'For me?' he looked at me pleadingly, not a look I recognised. Anyway, it didn't work.

'No, really. I'm knackered after that bike ride, and stiff! I need a hot bath more than a trip to the pub.'

'OK. Suit yourself.' He looked disappointed again. 'See ya.'

I kept thinking, oh no, not Cat and Gideon, but it was too late. There was nothing I could do about it. And it had been literally at the very moment I realised I'd fallen in love with him that I'd heard he was her boyfriend. The situation was too hideous.

I lay in the bath and thought about Gideon. It was as if he had suddenly shifted into sharp focus. I loved his wet-sand coloured hair and his grey eyes and his mysterious bearing. I loved his lanky form and his surfer's legs. Each one of the few things he'd said came back like stabs to my heart – 'I *said* she was good', 'Don't worry, Jo, I'll look after you.' Even 'Hi Jo,' and 'Don't mind him,' took on a new significance. But mostly it was our unspoken exchanges – the looks, catching his eye, not to mention the 'Annunciation'. He'd chosen *me*.

I washed my hair and dried it and then tried threading some of the little beads with shells on into it. It was bedlam in the cottage – my little cousins were over-excited and Tim was winding them up still further. I shut myself into my room. I don't normally go to bed at nine, but there was nowhere else I wanted to be.

I thought of sorting myself out with a list, but the facts of this matter didn't fit into lists. Cat had fallen for Gideon, the one guy in the whole of Cornwall that I had feelings for. She had no idea that I knew him personally, let alone that he meant anything to me.

I re-ran the images of her flinging her arms round him. I imagined the way her body and her energy would have felt to him. 'My new friend.' Oh yeah.

I day-dreamed for a bit that it wasn't true. If only he'd never met Cat. If only I'd taken him up on his offer of going to the pub with him on Saturday night. Maybe we would just have walked over the dunes instead, or along the sea. Maybe he would have told me again why he chose me to sing with him. Maybe he'd have held me. Maybe we'd have kissed. Oh why'd I spent time on that silly painting! At least it was going to be in his house. I wondered if he knew yet that I was the artist. I didn't know how Dad had entered it. Josie Liddell? Josephine Liddell? J. Liddell?

I imagined them all in the pub right now. (I tried *not* to imagine Cat and Gideon walking along by the sea.) What would they be saying about me? Would Tanya be there, slagging me off? Would Cat be dismissive? Would Seth or Ivan make the connection for her – that I knew Gideon and had sung with him?

And then, the worst images of all. I imagined Cat and Gideon together. I imagined them in the dunes. Like me and Matt. And sleep overtook me cruelly at that point, so that the world of my imagination became the world of my nightmares. Again and again I was forced to watch Cat and Gideon together and it was just like my memories of me and Matt where someone else seemed to be playing the part of Josie.

When I woke up it was morning, but there was no sun shining through my curtains. I looked at my watch. It was five am. I tried to get back to sleep, but I was wide awake. The images of Cat and Gideon slipped back into my mind. I knew I had to get up and do something, something that would chase the images away.

I tiptoed downstairs to fetch myself a drink. Taffy the yellow labrador was delighted to see me. She slid towards me, wagging her tail. She made little excited barking noises and then ran over to where her lead was hanging and jumped up at it. 'No, Taffy, it's too early,' I said. She frowned at me in that doggy way, and whimpered.

I tried to ignore her, and opened the fridge. I sat down with some orange juice, still ignoring her. But then she gave a little yap and I made the mistake of looking at her, and she got all enthusiastic again.

'Wait, Taffy,' I whispered. 'Wait until I put some clothes on. Lie down! Good girl!' and I crept upstairs to dress.

I unplugged the mobile from the charger, put it into my pocket and wrote a note. Then Taffy and I went out into the early morning. The washed sky was still pink from the sunrise, with pearly clouds. I walked down the long road to the sea. It was nice having the dog for company. She was well behaved on the road, not that there was any traffic, because she knew that soon she could hurtle over the dunes and along the beach. She knows me – she'll come back if I call her.

As we plodded along, the thoughts in my brain jogged about, trying to fall into some sort of pattern. I felt remorse about Matt, anxious about Cat, in love with Gideon, sick about Cat and Gideon – but there was no shape to these feelings, just jagged edges.

It took me nearly half an hour to get right down to the sea. I walked along the road past the pub, into the car park and up and over the dunes, where I let Taffy off the lead. It was absolutely gorgeous up there, a beautiful new day – no footprints in the sand below. I dropped down to the beach. Taffy had scrambled down ahead. The tide was a long way out. I kept on walking.

At low tide you can walk right round the headland to the bay. The tide was so far out I knew there was no danger of being cut off, and I could probably have climbed up into the dunes if necessary. I walked on, the prints left by my trainers in the sand looped and cut through again by small doggy ones. Usually the beach in the bay is full of families and small children, digging sandcastles, flying kites. Sometimes there are a few novice windsurfers, who spend more time in the water than skimming over it. On this fresh morning there was no one. I couldn't resist collecting the shells that were washed up on the sand – pearly razor shells, opalescent coils from tiny snails, mussel shells. Taffy ran wild on the empty beach. I would see her miles away and then she'd come racing back and off and away again.

By the time I reached the end of the bay where the car park is I must have walked for over an hour. But it was still early and glorious. There is a cliff path that runs from the car park over the top to the surfing beach. I felt fine with Taffy there, and though it was years since my mum and dad have been able to persuade me to do a cliff walk, I still remembered the exhilaration of the sky above and the sea below with only you and the pink thrift and yellow gorse in between. I sat on a bench looking out to sea for a few minutes. Taffy came and panted beside me. 'What d'you think, Taffs? Over the top?' It was seven am. I thought the cafe on the surfing beach would probably be open at seven thirty for a drink, and I had a bit of money in my pocket. Taffy ran round in little circles enthusiastically, so I took that as a 'yes' and we carried on along the cliff path.

Plod, plod, Gideon. Plod, plod, Cat. Plod, plod, Matt. Plod, plod, Cat and Gideon. Plod, plod, so unfair. Plod, plod, I can't bear it. Plod, plod, but Gideon's mine. Plod, plod, I can't bear the thought that the boy I love might be kissing my friend. Plod, plod, I can't bear the thought that my friend might be kissing the boy I love . . . BINGO!

I hurt so much, and yet I had it. This was how Cat must have felt. Because of me, Cat had felt like this. Only worse. Matt was already her boyfriend. And I'd known it.

The realisation was so terrible that I had to sit down. I cried real tears of shame and remorse. No *wonder* Cat hadn't wanted to speak to me Not if she'd felt like this. In Seth's words, I hadn't treated her as friends should treat one another.

Part of me wanted to run all the way home and throw myself on Cat and beg forgiveness. Maybe she had been going off Matt. Maybe it had all been a competition and maybe Matt was as much to blame as I was. Except that I was Cat's friend and I had betrayed that friendship.

I was a terrible person. There were no two ways about it.

Taffy came over and snuffled at me sympathetically. I hugged her and cried some more, and then I got up and walked on. The breeze off the sea blew my hair and I realised it was still beaded with shells. I must have looked a fright – no make-up, big hooded sweatshirt. The occasional dog-walker greeted me, but there was hardly anyone around.

I resolved to make it up with Cat. I so much didn't want to be that person any more – the girl who stole her best friend's boyfriend. I felt better for my resolve. But then, almost punching the wind out of me with the enormity of it – the thought of Cat and Gideon! Maybe I could just get on a train and go home. Forget Cornwall.

Cat and Gideon. The thought niggled me. How could I be sure that I was in love with Gideon for himself, and that it had nothing to do with him being Cat's boyfriend and therefore unavailable? It was no good. I needed to write a list. I felt in my pockets for a pencil or a biro and a receipt or something to write on. Nothing. There was no way down to the beach here. I was high up on the cliff path. I'd just have to speak it.

I half sung, half spoke my lists as I walked:

Reasons why I thought I was in love with Matt:
1) *He was good looking.*
2) *He was popular.*

3) *He was quite nice to me.*
4) *Because, because, he made a move on me.*

Oh, face it, Josie – you weren't in love with him at all. You just wanted to be accepted by the in-crowd. OK, OK, enough of this self-loathing.

Reasons why I think I'm in love with Gideon:
1) *I can't bear the thought of losing him to anyone, not just Cat.*
2) *He's so often been there and I've always noticed him and thought he was special.*
3) *Because he's good looking – well, I like his looks.*
4) *Because I feel he knows who I am.*

I stopped short. That was it! I felt that Gideon knew the real Josie, the real me.

And I was, I was in love with him. And he was going out with Cat.

I'd reached the top of the cliff. The early morning haze was lifting. The sea below was turquoise and the air smelt sweet and coconutty with gorse. I stood on the headland and stared out to sea, tears of remorse still trickling down my cheeks.

'Jo!'

I whipped round. It was Gideon.

'Jo? Are you OK?'

I didn't know what to say to that. But what was he doing here, right here, so early in the morning? 'What are you doing here?'

'I only live just over there.' He pointed inland, and I

realised that, of course, that's where the Elliott's house was. 'And I was on the look-out for dolphins. We're doing a sort of unscientific survey for my grandfather – you know – when, where, how many . . .'

'Have you seen any today?'

'No – I think evenings are better.' He looked at my tear-stained face. 'Hey, Jo, are you sure you're OK?'

I grunted something non-committal.

'Anyway, what are *you* doing out here at this time of the morning?'

Taffy came panting up to us. 'Walking the dog.'

'And that makes you unhappy?'

'No. I'm unhappy about something else.'

'OK,' he said cheerfully. 'None of my business. I won't ask.'

'Thanks.' I couldn't believe Gideon was here, beside me. My knees felt weak, my heart was thumping and my stomach was full of butterflies.

'Are you going to carry on walking round the cliff, or are you going back?' Gideon asked. A perfectly reasonable question.

'I – I don't know.'

He pushed back his hair and looked me in the eye. 'Well, I'm going back to my house for breakfast, and if you want to come with me I'm sure someone will give you a lift home.'

I thought about it. I'd been going to phone Dad at some point and ask for a lift. No one from my family had called the mobile, though actually the signal wasn't that good on the cliff. All I wanted to say to Gideon was, 'Forget Cat, go out with me.' The words were going round in my head so fiercely I was afraid I'd say them out loud by mistake. 'All right,' was what came out.

'You can have breakfast with us if you like.'

Taffy and I followed him home. When we arrived, Eileen put out a bowl of water for Taffy and she gulped it down. 'Hello, Jo,' she said. 'We're just about to hang the painting. Tell your father we're delighted, especially Caleb, of course.'

I sat down at the kitchen table. Ebbie was roaring round. 'Hello Virgin!' he said.

'Still not funny, Ebz,' said Gideon.

'That's enough, Ebbie,' said Eileen. 'You can watch the grand picture-hanging if you like, Jo, and then report back home. It's going on Caleb's landing, naturally.'

I looked at Gideon, confused.

'Caleb's the big surfer round here. I do it too, but he's almost a professional. And he fell in love with your dad's painting. And then Cat's parents were going to buy it, but Cat persuaded them that Caleb should have it – and saved them some money.'

'Worth it though,' said Eileen. 'I imagine your father's paintings normally fetch thousands, don't they?'

I drank the coffee and ate the croissant put in front of me without remembering that I don't much like coffee, apart from the smell, and I usually have butter and jam with croissants. Caleb appeared, looking chirpy.

'Spare us!' said Gideon, before Caleb could say anything.

'I was just going to comment on the fact that we have the daughter of the guy who painted my fabuloso surfing painting, and—'

'I'm just going to phone home,' I said. 'I left a note, but they might be wondering where I've got to.'

'Fine, phone's in the hall,' said Gideon.

'No, it's OK, I'll just take the mobile outside.' I stood outside the kitchen door. 'Dad? Hi, it's me. I bumped into Gideon Elliott and they've given me breakfast. Any chance of a lift?' Dad said he'd be over in twenty minutes.

Gideon had been listening. 'I said we'd give you a lift. I thought you might stay a bit.'

I looked at him. 'Gideon? There's a lot of confusion going around. Do you think we could talk?'

'Sure,' he said. 'What sort of confusion?'

We sat down on the bench outside the kitchen. 'OK, one: you, Cat and the painting. Who was it for, precisely?'

'Caleb.'

'Cat wanted it for Caleb?'

'Well, I think it's cool, too, but it's Caleb's sort of thing, pictures of surfers.'

'Two: have you looked closely at the painting, and seen what it's actually of?'

'It's not up yet.'

'It's a picture of dolphins. There's only one human in it.'

'Ha! Don't tell Caleb, then.'

'Three: what makes you think the painting is by my dad?'

'Mum said it was by J. Liddell, tenor in the choir. She even checked the concert programme.'

'Have you still got the programme?'

'Yeah. I think I've even got one scrumpled up in the pocket of this jacket.' He pulled it out. 'Here!'

'Just point out J. Liddell to me, would you?'

'What's all this about, Jo?'

I didn't quite know why I was spinning all this out, either, but it seemed important to get everything, all the mix-ups, absolutely straight, because I was beginning to think that the biggest mix-up of all was going to change everything. I pointed to my name under *Alto* in the Barnes Annunciation: Josephine Liddell.

Gideon looked at it and then looked at me. 'You mean—'

'It's my painting. And it's dolphins, with one boy. Have a look at him when it's up. And don't tell the others yet, they might think they've been fleeced if it's a kid's painting.'

'*Your* painting?' His eyes were gratifyingly wide.

'Four: what's going on between—' I hardly dared ask the question in case the answer wasn't what I wanted to hear – 'Caleb and Cat?'

'Well – they – seemed to click. And they've only got four days left so they're making the most of it. Any more confusions?'

The smile I turned on him almost cracked my face. I couldn't manage the tight-lipped, hide-the-brace one. 'No,' I said. 'None whatsoever. Thank you.' I heard my dad's car arriving. I didn't want the Elliotts to button-hole him about the painting, so I put Taffy on her lead and asked Gideon to say thanks to his mum for break-fast.

'Hey!' he shouted after me. 'Round about eight this evening there might be dolphins!'

Dad drove off. 'Perhaps you'd like to tell me what all this is about?' he said.

'Guess what, Dad?'

'Can't.'

'The Elliotts think my painting was done by you. Mrs Elliott thinks she's got a bargain and that your paintings must normally fetch thousands!'

'Great!' Dad laughed. 'Well, they won't be able to hound me today because we're having a family outing to Heligan. A treat for Mum. Bring your sketchbook!'

'But that's a garden. Dad. How did you manage to persuade Tim to come?'

'Partly by reminding him that another family is doing the same outing today – a family of girls with long names.'

'Oh, Cleopatra and Bathsheba?'

'And Tallulah, apparently.'

'Nearly as bad as the Elliotts. Perhaps Tallulah and Ebenezer will get together some day.' I felt ridiculously happy. 'Tim must be smitten if he'll go to a garden for Cleo.'

'It's quite a place. You and Tim will both be pleasantly surprised I think.'

'When will we be back?'

'Oh, don't worry. Long before eight pm.' He winked at me.

'There's something important I have to do before that, Dad. I'll come if we can be home by six.'

'Done.'

Fourteen

True to his word, Dad got us back at five to six. I'd spent most of my time at Heligan sitting in the jungle bit working up a tendrilly design of flowers. As soon as we got in I dug out one of the little frames Dad had bought along with the big one for my painting and put the picture into it. I took it up the hill with me to Cat's. Her mum told me I'd find her in her bedroom.

'Cat?'

'Hi, Josie.' She was gazing dreamily out of the window.

'I've come to say sorry, properly.'

'Oh?'

'It's taken me this long to realise how I must have made you feel.'

'Completely ghastly, humiliated, suicidal, you mean?'

'All those. I can't believe I – I mean, being friends with you is more important than – and I – Matt was your boyfriend, you know? – and I—'

'Yeah, well. I was pretty hacked off with you. Just the thought of my friend and my boyfriend—'

'I know, I know. I'm sorry. Look, this is a sort of peace offering.' I handed her the picture.

'Ooh, cool. It looks like a tattoo!'

I hadn't thought of that. 'I'll draw one on you if you like. Got a biro?'

'Brilliant. I want it just above my left boob, so Caleb gets a tantalising glimpse of it . . .'

'So it's cool with Caleb?'

'Totally. And don't you dare . . .'

'Never again, Cat.'

The tattoo looked great. 'Are you seeing Caleb tonight?'

'Of course. He's meeting me down the pub at seven thirty, though I dare say we won't stay there all evening.'

'And your parents don't mind?'

'They're terribly impressed by the Elliotts – famous conductor, all that art. By the way, did you see Caleb's painting? My mum and dad nearly bought it for me, but it was perfect for him. I don't usually like that sort of thing, but I did like that one.'

'Yes,' I said. 'I saw it.'

'I really wanted him to have it.' She gave me one of her sly Cat looks. 'Hey, Josie. I like him much better than Matt. There were times when Matt didn't seem really interested in me as a person, just what he could make me do with him. That's what we quarrelled about. It was almost as if he was trying to score points. I suggested that and he got really angry.'

'Perish the thought.'

'D'you want to come down to the pub with us?' Cat asked. 'I can't wait to see Caleb's face when he sees this. I bet he thinks it's real.'

'I might come along later, but there's something I want to see at eight.'

'I wouldn't know what's on TV – we haven't got one here.'

I didn't fill her in. 'Maybe see you later, then. If not – beach tomorrow?'

'Whatever. I'll call for you.'

'So I suppose you'll be wanting a lift to the Elliotts?'

'How did you know? Actually, the bit of the cliff path nearest their house.'

'And how are you going to get home?'

'I'll take the mobile, if that's OK.'

'Come on, then.'

Dad dropped me off. It was perfectly light and there were people around, though he took some persuading that I'd be all right even if I didn't meet up with Gideon.

I climbed up the steps that led to this bit of cliff path. It was a gorgeous evening – the colours were fabulous. I ran up, anxious at the point before the steps turned the corner that I'd got it all wrong and Gideon wouldn't be there.

I reached the top. There was the headland. And there was Gideon staring out to sea. I went up to him. 'Hi!' I said quietly.

He turned to me and took my hand as if he'd known I would come to him. We listened to the surf crashing below. 'I think I'm slightly afraid of you, Jo,' he said, not looking at me.

'Me? Why?'

'Because you're so – so. Well, that painting! It's brilliant. And I did look at the boy. And I—'

'Coming from someone who's already a prodigy—'

'Jo – I've never been crazy about anyone before. I'm crazy about you, and I've never felt like this. It's new. It's kind of awesome, scary.'

I suffered a moment of horror, thinking the scary part might be snogging a girl with a brace, but Gideon didn't flinch. 'Not with me it won't be,' I tried to soothe him. We were gazing into each other's eyes. We'd been here before.

Gideon took both my hands in his. 'The boy was me, wasn't it?'

'Of course.'

And then we kissed. We'd reached the love part.

I had my arm round Gideon's waist. He was stroking my hair. We were both watching the sea. Suddenly – 'Yay!' he yelled. And there they were, three of them, leaping.

I have never seen anything like it. The sight of dolphins playing simply fills your heart with joy, there is no other way to describe it.

'They're doing it for us,' said Gideon, rubbing my cheek with his. I felt his silky hair on my face, and neither of us knew whether to kiss again or watch the dolphins – a dilemma which could be a definition of happiness! We sort of managed to do both until we realised we were surrounded by quite a crowd of people all pointing at the dolphins.

'Shall we walk over the cliffs to the pub?' Gideon asked. 'Caleb will be there. With Cat,' he said, squeezing my shoulder.

'It depends on the tide at the bay doesn't it?'

'We can go over the top there, too.'

We set off, holding hands. I wanted to know when he'd first noticed me and he wanted to hear all about me worrying that he was the one Cat fancied. I told him how cool he'd seemed and he said he thought I was much more interesting than the rest of that crowd – 'though I like Seth,' he said.

'Seth's my mate,' I said.

'And mine,' said Gideon. 'He'll kill me.'

'Why?'

'Because – he's – kind of proprietary about you. But you must know that?'

'I don't want to think about it.' I didn't.

Gideon's fingers caught in my dolphin bracelet. He lifted my wrist. 'Hey, it's the same as mine!'

'I know. I saw yours when I first noticed you and Caleb outside the pub. I suppose you were looking for dolphins?' Gideon nodded. 'And when I found the last bracelet in the shop I had to have it. You see, I thought you were kind of magic from the first time I saw you.' He looked at me with the sea-grey gaze. 'And you always will be.'

The tide was out round the headland of the bay, and still going out, so we splashed our way across. It was almost dark and a moon was rising, but we made out two more people splashing and giggling further round.

'Oh great,' said Gideon. 'My brother. So they're not at the pub.'

Cat and Caleb were larking about. We'd both had the same idea, except we were going in opposite directions. I pulled Gideon back behind a rock. 'Actually, I'd rather just be with you tonight. We can all four be together tomorrow.'

'Actually,' he said, 'so would I.' We let them go past the way we'd arrived.

'Cat's a laugh,' said Gideon, 'but she's not my type.'

'That's lucky.'

At some point my phone rang – Dad checking up on me.

In fact we were both cold and it was late, so I let Dad pick us up and run Gideon home. We arrived at the same time as Cat and Caleb, so we gave her a lift back too. It all felt so civilised and easy compared with last week. I got in the back with Cat. 'Sorry, chauffeur,' I said to Dad. 'Cat and I have a lot of catching up to do.'

The next day, Friday, was our last full day, Cat's too. We spent it on the surfing beach. Everyone was there, all the parents, Seth, Archie and Harry, Tim, everyone. Cat surfed with the boys. I stayed back with the girls. My relationship with Gideon was too new to be public and so was Cat's with Caleb, so Seth was spared and so was poor old Harry, though Liza and Tanya were taking quite an interest all of a sudden in this good-looking guy, earring and all. Ivan was as creepy as ever, but even he felt like someone we'd miss tomorrow.

Talking of which . . . The thought of leaving Gideon was ghastly. I spent quite a lot of our last evening together feeling weepy. He was pretty wobbly, too. We were on the bench on the cliff path. 'I'll nip up and look at your painting every day,' he said. 'And there's a recording of the Barnes. I'll listen to that. There'll be a copy for you, by the way.'

'Thanks,' I sniffed. 'Gideon?'

'Yes?'

'There's something I'll never understand.'

'What's that?'

'You don't seem to mind my brace.'

'Why should I? It's just another part of my beautiful Jo. If you haven't got it next year I'll quite miss it.'

'Do you think we'll survive until next year?'

'I'll be very upset if we don't.' And then we started kissing again. And we didn't stop until my phone rang and Dad said he was waiting in the car park for me with Cat.

Gideon gulped. 'So it's goodbye, then,' and we clutched at each other desperately, all tears and hair and final kisses, until I had to pull away and run to the car.

We were leaving pretty early. Cat's parents were packing up at the same time as mine, so Cat and I spent the last hour or so chatting together. We really were friends again. 'I still want to know,' she said, 'what made you finally realise how I'd felt when I heard about you and Matt. Go on, tell me – you owe me.'

'I wasn't going to, but I suppose it's only fair. You see, I started to get a thing about Gideon after the concert. I didn't know quite what I felt about him. Then I suddenly realised that I really, really wanted him, far more than I'd wanted Matt. And then almost straight away I found out that you were interested in one of the Elliott boys, and I assumed it was Gideon. I couldn't stop imagining the two of you together. I went to hell and back. And then I realised that you must have felt like that about me and Matt – only worse. So I – well, I reckon this holiday's taught me a lot.'

Cat cuffed me affectionately. 'Idiot!' was all she said.

'Do you think we'll still be going out with the Elliotts next year?' I asked, to dispel the slight awkwardness.

'Dunno,' said Cat. 'It partly depends who else I meet.' I couldn't agree. Gideon was there in my subconscious – he was there at every level. He'd be there, somewhere, all my life. 'Maybe, one year,' Cat said, 'Seth will get a chance.'

'Oh thanks Cat. And you'll give Harry a chance too?'

'Well, who knows?' she said. 'That's the great thing – there'll always be next year.'

'Are you *ever* going to stop gassing and help pack, Josie?' Mum called, exasperated.

'OK, Mum. So where's Tim?'

'We're picking him up from Cleo's. Last-minute fare-well.'

Seth, Harry, Archie, Liza, Tanya – and even Ivan – managed to get out of bed and wave to Cat's family and mine as we drove off. I was kind of glad Gideon and I had said our goodbyes last night – it meant I could savour them in private.

On the way home I wrote a final Cornwall list. Just the good things:

> <u>Good things about Cornwall</u>
> The sea
> The cliffs
> The cottage
> The music
> My friends: Seth, Harry, Archie, Liza, Tanya, Ivan (just).
> My best friend: Cat.
> My boyfriend: Gideon.
> Coming here every year.

And that just about said it all, really.

Epilogue

The journey home took forever. Tim and Cleo had disappeared, so we had to wait, making polite conversation with Bathsheba and Tallulah and their parents until they returned. Then it took ages to get lunch at the motorway service station. And then, most frustrating of all, we had to stop off at Granny's and eat tea and tell her everything. We didn't walk in the front door until after eleven pm and we were all tired and crotchety.

'Bags the phone first!' I yelled, not that anyone else was going to use it at that time of night. I rang Holly and prayed that she hadn't gone to bed. She hadn't. 'Hey Holly, you'll never guess what—'

But she stopped me and said I should save it for tomorrow night. Quite a good thing, perhaps. It gave me more time to think about all the things that had happened. I thought I'd tell them about Matt as well as Gideon, almost to punish myself I suppose. Though when I think about the competition the boys themselves were having, I don't feel quite so bad. Nor, with a bit of distance between us, would I put Cat past doing the same thing to me in those circumstances.

Holly and I arrived at Zoe's house together, just after Alex. It was great being back with the other three. Zoe practically has her own flat in the basement and there's always masses of food – it's a bit like going to a self-service restaurant. We loaded up with food and then – da-dum! It was time for us all to report back. I wouldn't have minded kicking off, but Alex was absolutely bursting to tell us, so Zoe made us go in alphabetical order.

So, Alex. Alex the tomboy. Alex the tomboy no longer, it seemed! She even looked different. I have to admit I never thought Alex would have a romance to report on, but she certainly did. And she seemed to have grown up a lot in the process. I started to worry about how my story was going to sound.

Then Holly told us what had happened to her. I was quite shocked when I heard that she'd done the best-friend's boyfriend thing too, only the other way round! The stately home sounded brilliant though, and it's typical of Holly that if she goes off one guy, it's never long before she finds another one who fancies her.

Suddenly it was my turn. I'd already decided I would tell them about Matt, though the more I tried to explain the complicated situation, the worse it sounded! I even wondered if it was because we'd all promised to have romances that I'd behaved so badly, but I don't think anyone agreed with me! And then when it came to the music and Gideon – I couldn't quite find the words. It was all too recent. Still, I'm sure we'll all talk more later on, especially Holly and me.

And then it was Zoe's turn. Sometimes Zoe just seems so grown-up. The way she described what had happened to her, and the voyage of self-discovery she had been on, made my silly little episode with Matt seem so trivial! Like the others I listened to her wide-eyed. But then I thought about Gideon and me and remembered that our feelings for each other were incredibly profound. We had managed to express ourselves at a deeper level than words. And how many people could say that?

It was time to write some more lists, private ones.

Also in the *GIRLS LIKE YOU SERIES*:

Sophie

Blonde, drop-dead beautiful Sophie is used to getting her own way, and not worrying about the broken hearts she leaves behind. She's determined that a family camping holiday in France is not going to cramp her style. What's more she knows exactly who she wants . . . but does he feel the same way about her?

Hannah

Hannah is the clever one, and hard to please – but she's really shy too. She doesn't fancy her chances on a summer music course – so she decides that the boys are just not worth bothering about . . . not any of them . . . or are they?

Charlotte

Shy, dreamy Charlotte has been going to the Lake District every year for as long as she can remember and she's loved Josh from afar for as long. But this year she's doing without her older sister. It might be the chance she's been waiting for. What if Josh notices her – just because she's four years younger than him – it doesn't mean all her dreams won't come true – does it?

Maddy

Finding romance has never been a problem for Maddy – she's always been a beauty and dramatic with it. So she can't wait for her exotic holiday in Barbados with Dad – it's going to be brilliant, and so different from life at home with impoverished Mum. The stage is set – but is romance all that lies in store for Maddy?

Alex

With four brothers at home, Alex has always been one of the lads. Not for her all this starry-eyed romance stuff. Every summer she plays in a tennis tournament. This year it's the under 16s – and mixed doubles partners really matter. Suddenly Alex finds it's not her tennis technique she's concentrating on – and she's more determined than ever to win a different sort of match.

Holly

Holly is already in love – with Jonty, the boy she met in Barbados this summer. Now she's on her way to stay with them at the family's country estate – complete with tennis courts and racehorses – it sounds like a dream but will it turn out to be a nightmare?

Zoe

The last thing smart, beautiful Zoe wanted to spend the last precious days of her summer holiday doing was taking her little brother to the local Community Theatre Project. But waiting in the wings is the mysterious, exciting, unpredictable Lennie and Zoe is swept off her feet by him and his passion for the Project. If only he could burn with the same passion for her. Zoe decides to make it happen – but the results aren't quite what she expected.